"Surely There... You'd Be ... To Inspire Me T...

"I…don't know what you mean."

"My hypothetical marriage to your sister is a business deal, after all. As a businessman, I would require compensation for letting the deal fall through."

Quinn's blue eyes stung her, causing the pulse in her throat to hammer frantically.

"Maybe…er…the satisfaction of doing a good deed for once in your life?" Kira said.

He laughed. "That's a refreshing idea if ever I heard one—but, like most humans I'm driven by the desire to avoid pain and pursue pleasure."

"And to think—I imagined you to be primarily driven by greed. Well, I don't have any money."

"I don't want your money."

"What do you want then?"

"I think you know," he said silkily, leaning closer.

* * *

Dear Reader,

Stories are the imaginary children of a writer's soul.
I tend to write about family, the need to belong and
loneliness.

My heroine, Kira, needs to feel she belongs to her family.
There's no sacrifice she won't make in that endeavor. To
save her sister, she'll even marry a man whose lifelong
goal has been the destruction of her family.

As in real life, when all too often the most mysterious
forces in our lives are the yearnings hidden deep within
our own hearts that drive us, Kira doesn't know where
her feelings come from until she discovers a long-kept
family secret. Fortunately, by then she is in love with her
new husband and is loved in return.

Enjoy,

Ann Major

ANN MAJOR

TERMS OF ENGAGEMENT

Recycling programs
for this product may
not exist in your area.

ISBN-13: 978-0-373-73144-2

TERMS OF ENGAGEMENT

Books by Ann Major

Harlequin Desire

Marriage at the Cowboy's Command #2101
Terms of Engagement #2131

Silhouette Desire

Midnight Fantasy #1304
Cowboy Fantasy #1375
A Cowboy & a Gentleman #1477
Shameless #1513
The Bride Tamer #1586
The Amalfi Bride #1784
Sold into Marriage #1832
Mistress for a Month #1869
The Throw-Away Bride #1912
The Bride Hunter #1945
To Tame Her Tycoon Lover #1984
Ultimatum: Marriage #2041

*Golden Spurs

MIRA Books

The Girl with the Golden Spurs
The Girl with the Golden Gun
The Secret Lives of Doctors' Wives

Other titles by this author available in ebook

ANN MAJOR

lives in Texas with her husband of many years and is the mother of three grown children. She has a master's degree from Texas A&M at Kingsville, Texas, and is a former English teacher. She is a founding board member of the Romance Writers of America and a frequent speaker at writers' groups.

Ann loves to write—she considers her ability to do so a gift. Her hobbies include hiking in the mountains, sailing, ocean kayaking, traveling and playing the piano. But most of all, she enjoys her family. Visit her website at www.annmajor.com.

To Ted, with all my love.

And as always I must thank my editor, Stacy Boyd, and Shana Smith, along with the entire Harlequin Desire team for their talented expertise.
I thank as well my agent, Karen Solem.

One

No good deed goes unpunished.

When would she ever learn? Kira wondered.

With her luck, never.

So, here she sat, in the office of oil billionaire Quinn Sullivan, too nervous to concentrate on her magazine as she waited to see if he would make time for a woman he probably thought of as just another adversary to be crushed in his quest for revenge.

Dreadful, arrogant man.

If he did grant her an audience, would she have any chance of changing his mind about destroying her family's company, Murray Oil, and forcing her sister Jaycee into marriage?

A man vengeful enough to hold a grudge against her father for twenty years couldn't possibly have a heart that could be swayed.

Kira Murray clenched and unclenched her hands. Then

she sat on them, twisting in her chair. When the man across from her began to stare, she told herself to quit squirming. Lowering her eyes to her magazine, she pretended to read a very boring article on supertankers.

High heels clicked rapidly on marble, causing Kira to look up in panic.

"Miss Murray, I'm so sorry. I was wrong. Mr. Sullivan *is* still here." There was surprise in his secretary's classy, soothing purr.

"In fact, he'll see you now."

"He will?" Kira squeaked. *"Now?"*

The secretary's answering smile was a brilliant white.

Kira's own mouth felt as dry as sandpaper. She actually began to shake. To hide this dreadful reaction, she jumped to her feet so fast she sent the glossy magazine to the floor, causing the man across from her to glare in annoyance.

Obviously, she'd been hoping Quinn would refuse to see her. A ridiculous wish when she'd come here for the express purpose of finally meeting him properly and having her say.

Sure, she'd run into him once, informally. It had been right after he'd announced he wanted to marry one of the Murray daughters to make his takeover of Murray Oil less hostile. Her father had suggested Jaycee, and Kira couldn't help but think he'd done so because Jaycee was his favorite and most biddable daughter. As always, Jaycee had dutifully agreed with their father's wishes, so Quinn had come to the ranch for a celebratory dinner to seal the bargain.

He'd been late. A man as rich and arrogant as he was probably thought himself entitled to run on his own schedule.

Wounded by her mother's less-than-kind assessment of her outfit when she'd first arrived—"Jeans and a torn shirt? How could you think that appropriate for meeting a man so important to this family's welfare?"—Kira had stormed out of the house. She hadn't had time to change after the crisis at her best friend's restaurant, where Kira was temporarily waiting tables while looking for a museum curator position. Since her mother always turned a deaf ear to Kira's excuses, rather than explain, Kira had decided to walk her dad's hunting spaniels while she nursed her injured feelings.

The brilliant, red sun that had been sinking fast had been in her eyes as the spaniels leaped onto the gravel driveway, dragging her in their wake. Blinded, she'd neither seen nor heard Quinn's low-slung, silver Aston Martin screaming around the curve. Slamming on his brakes, he'd veered clear of her with several feet to spare. She'd tripped over the dogs and fallen into a mud puddle.

Yipping wildly, the dogs had raced back to the house, leaving her to face Quinn on her own with cold, dirty water dripping from her chin.

Quinn had gotten out of his fancy car and stomped over in his fancy Italian loafers just as she got to her feet. For a long moment, he'd inspected every inch of her. Then, mindless of her smudged face, chattering teeth and muddy clothes, he'd pulled her against his tall, hard body, making her much too aware of his clean, male smell and hard, muscular body.

"Tell me you're okay."

He was tall and broad-shouldered, so tall he'd towered over her. His angry blue eyes had burned her; his viselike fingers had cut into her elbow. Despite his overcharged emotions, she'd liked being in his arms—liked it too much.

"Damn it, I didn't hit you, did I? Well, say something, why don't you?"

"How can I—with you yelling at me?"

"Are you okay, then?" he asked, his grip loosening, his

voice softening into a husky sound so unexpectedly beautiful she'd shivered. This time, she saw concern in his hard expression.

Had it happened then?

Oh, be honest, Kira, at least with yourself. That was the moment you formed an inappropriate crush on your sister's future fiancé, a man whose main goal in life is to destroy your family.

He'd been wearing faded jeans, a white shirt, his sleeves rolled up to his elbows. On her, jeans looked rumpled, but on him, jeans had made him ruggedly, devastatingly handsome. Over one arm, he carried a cashmere jacket.

She noted his jet-black hair and carved cheekbones with approval. Any woman would have. His skin had been darkly bronzed, and the dangerous aura of sensuality surrounding him had her sizzling.

Shaken by her fall and by the fact that *the enemy* was such an attractive, powerful man who continued to hold her close and stare down at her with blazing eyes, her breath had come in fits and starts.

"I said—*are you okay?*"

"I was fine—until you grabbed me." Her hesitant voice was tremulous…and sounded strangely shy. "You're hurting me, really hurting me!" She'd lied so he would let her go, and yet part of her hadn't wanted to be released.

His eyes narrowed suspiciously. "Sorry," he'd said, his tone harsh again.

"Who the hell are you anyway?" he'd demanded.

"Nobody important," she'd muttered.

His dark brows winged upward. "Wait…I've seen your pictures… You're the older sister. The waitress."

"Only temporarily…until I get a new job as a curator."

"Right. You were fired."

"So, you've heard Father's version. The truth is, my professional opinion wasn't as important to the museum director as I might have liked, but I was let go due to budget constraints."

"Your sister speaks highly of you."

"Sometimes I think she's the only one in this family who does."

Nodding as if he understood, he draped his jacket around her shoulders. "I've wanted to meet you." When she glanced up at him, he said, "You're shivering. The least I can do is offer you my jacket and a ride back to the house."

Her heart pounded much too fast, and she was mortified that she was covered with mud and that she found her family's enemy exciting and the prospect of wearing his jacket a thrill. Not trusting herself to spend another second with such a dangerous man, especially in the close quarters of his glamorous car, she'd shaken her head. "I'm too muddy."

"Do you think I give a damn about that? I could have killed you."

"You didn't. So let's just forget about it."

"Not possible! Now, put my jacket on before you catch your death."

Pulling his jacket around her shoulders, she turned on her heel and left him. Nothing had happened, she'd told herself as she stalked rapidly through the woods toward the house.

Nothing except the enemy she'd feared had held her and made her feel dangerously alive in a way no other man ever had.

When she'd reached the house, she'd been surprised to find him outside waiting for her as he held on to her yapping dogs. Feeling tingly and shyly thrilled as he handed her their tangled leashes, she'd used her muddy clothes again as an excuse to go home and avoid dinner, when her father would formally announce Quinn was to marry her sister.

Yes, he was set on revenge against those she loved most, but that hadn't been the reason she couldn't sit across the table from him. No, it was her crush. How could she have endured such a dinner when just to look at him made her skin heat?

For weeks after that chance meeting, her inappropriate attachment to Quinn had continued to claim her, causing her much guilt-ridden pain. She'd thought of him constantly. And more than once, before she'd returned his jacket to Jaycee, she'd worn it around her apartment, draped over her shoulders, just because his scent lingered on the soft fabric.

Now, retrieving the magazine she'd dropped, she set it carefully on the side table. Then she sucked in a deep breath. Not that it steadied her nerves.

No. Instead, her heart raced when Quinn Sullivan's secretary turned away, saying, "Follow me."

Kira swallowed. She'd put this interview off to the last possible moment—to the end of the business day—because she'd been trying to formulate a plan to confront a man as powerful and dictatorial and, yes, as dangerously sexy, as Quinn Sullivan.

But she hadn't come up with a plan. Did she ever have a plan? She'd be at a disadvantage since Sullivan planned everything down to the last detail, including taking his revenge plot up a notch by marrying Jaycee.

Kira had to sprint to keep up with the sleek, blonde secretary, whose ridiculous, four-inch, ice-pick, gold heels clicked on the polished gray marble. Did *he* make the poor girl wear such gaudy, crippling footwear?

Quinn's waiting room with its butter-soft leather couches and polished wainscoting had reeked of old money. In truth, he was nothing but a brash, bad-tempered upstart. His long hallway, decorated with paintings of vivid mini-malistic splashes of color, led to what would probably prove to be an obscenely opulent office. Still, despite her wish to dislike everything about him, she admired the art and wished she could stop and study several of the pictures. They were elegant, tasteful and interesting. Had he selected them himself?

Probably not. He was an arrogant show-off.

After their one encounter, she'd researched him. It seemed he believed her father had profited excessively when he'd bought Quinn's father out of their mutually owned company. In addition, he blamed her father for his father's suicide—if suicide it had been.

Quinn, who'd known hardship after his father's death, was determined to make up for his early privations, by living rich and large. Craving glamour and the spotlight, he never attended a party without a beauty even more daz-zling than his secretary on his arm.

He was a respected art collector. In various interviews he'd made it clear nobody would ever look down on him again. Not in business; not in his personal life. He was king of his kingdom.

From the internet, she'd gleaned that Quinn's bedroom had a revolving door. Apparently, a few nights' pleasur-ing the same woman were more than enough for him. Just when a woman might believe she meant something to him, he'd drop her and date another gorgeous blonde, who was invariably more beautiful than the one he'd jilted. There had been one woman, also blonde, who'd jilted him a year or so ago, a Cristina somebody. Not that she hadn't been quickly forgotten by the press when he'd resumed chasing more beauties as carelessly as before.

From what Kira had seen, his life was about winning,

not about caring deeply. For that purpose only, he'd surrounded himself with the mansions, the cars, the yachts, the art collections and the fair-haired beauties. She had no illusions about what his marriage to Jaycee would be like. He had no intention of being a faithful husband to Kira's beautiful, blonde sister.

Rich, handsome womanizer that he was, Kira might have pitied him for being cursed with such a dark heart—if only her precious Jaycee wasn't central in his revenge scheme.

Kira was not gifted at planning or at being confrontational, which were two big reasons why she wasn't getting ahead in her career. And Quinn was the last person on earth she wanted to confront. But the need to take care of Jaycee, as she had done since her sister's birth, was paramount.

Naturally, Kira's first step had been to beg her father to change his mind about using her sister to smooth over a business deal, but her father had been adamant about the benefits of the marriage.

Kira didn't understand the financials of Quinn's hostile takeover of Murray Oil, but her father seemed to think Quinn would make a brilliant CEO. Her parents had said that if Jaycee didn't walk down the aisle with Quinn as agreed, Quinn's terms would become far more onerous. Not to mention that the employees would resent him as an outsider. Even though Quinn's father had been a co-owner, Quinn was viewed as a man with a personal vendetta against the Murrays and Murray Oil. Ever since his father's death, rumors about his hostility toward all things Murray had been widely circulated by the press. Only if he married Jaycee would the employees believe that peace between the two families had at last been achieved and that the company would be safe in his hands.

Hence, Kira was here, to face Quinn Sullivan.

She was determined to stop him from marrying Jaycee, but how? Pausing in panic even as his secretary rushed ahead, she reminded herself that she couldn't turn back, plan or not.

Quickening her pace, Kira caught up to the efficient young woman, who was probably moving so quickly because she was as scared of the unfeeling brute as Kira was.

When his secretary pushed open Quinn's door, the deep, rich tones of the man's surprisingly beautiful voice moved through Kira like music. Her knees lost strength, and she stopped in midstep.

Oh, no, it was happening again.

She'd known from meeting him the first time that he was charismatic, but she'd counted on her newly amassed knowledge of his despicable character to protect her. His edgy baritone slid across her nerve endings, causing warm tingles in her secret, feminine places, and she knew she was as vulnerable to him as before.

Fighting not to notice that her nipples ached and that her pulse had sped up, she took a deep breath before daring a glance at the black-headed rogue. Looking very much at ease, he sat sprawled at his desk, the back of his linebacker shoulders to her as he leaned against his chair, a telephone jammed to his ear.

She couldn't, wouldn't, be attracted to this man.

On his desk she noted a silver-framed photograph of his father. With their intense blue eyes, black hair and strongly chiseled, tanned features, father and son closely resembled each other. Both, she knew, had been college athletes. Did Quinn keep the photo so close out of love or to energize him in his quest for revenge?

"I told you to buy, Habib," he ordered brusquely in that

too-beautiful voice. "What's there to talk about? Do it."
He ended the call.

At least he was every bit as rude as she remembered.
Deep baritone or not, it should be easy to hate him.

His secretary coughed to let him know they were at the
door.

Quinn whirled around in his massive, black leather
chair, scowling, but went still the instant he saw Kira.

He lifted that hard, carved chin, which surprisingly
enough had the most darling dimple, and, just like that,
dismissed his secretary.

His piercing, laser-blue gaze slammed into Kira full
force and heated her through—just like before.

Black hair. Bronze skin. Fierce, brilliant eyes… With a
single glance the man bewitched her.

When his mouth lifted at the edges, her world shifted as
it had that first evening—and he hadn't even touched her.

He was as outrageously handsome as ever. Every bit as
dark, tall, lean and hard, as cynical and untamed—even
in his orderly office with his efficient secretary standing
guard.

Still, for an instant, Kira thought she saw turbulent grief
and longing mix with unexpected pleasure at the sight of
her.

He remembered her.

But in a flash the light went out of his eyes, and his
handsome features tightened into those of the tough, heart-
less man he wanted people to see.

In spite of his attempt at distance, a chord of recognition
had been struck. It was as if they'd seen into each other's
souls, had sensed each other's secret yearnings.

She wanted her family, who deemed her difficult and
frustrating, to love and accept her for herself, as they did
her sister.

He had longings that revenge and outward success had failed to satisfy. What were they? What was lacking in his disciplined, showy, materialistic life?

Was he as drawn to her as she was to him?

Impossible.

So how could he be the only man who'd ever made her feel less alone in the universe?

Hating him even more because he'd exposed needs she preferred to conceal, she tensed. He had no right to open her heart and arouse such longings.

Frowning, he cocked his dark head and studied her. "I owe you an apology for the last time we met," he drawled in that slow, mocking baritone that turned her insides to mush. "I was nervous about the takeover and the engagement and about making a good impression on you and your family. I was too harsh with you. A few inches more…and I could have killed you. I was afraid, and that made me angry."

"You owe me nothing," she said coolly.

"I don't blame you in the least for avoiding me all these weeks. I probably scared the hell out of you."

"I haven't been avoiding you. Not really," she murmured, but a telltale flush heated her neck as she thought of the family dinners she'd opted out of because she'd known he'd be there.

If only she could run now, escape him. But Jaycee needed her, so instead, she hedged. "I've been busy."

"Waitressing?"

"Yes! I'm helping out Betty, my best friend, while I interview for museum jobs. Opening a restaurant on the San Antonio River Walk was a lifetime dream of hers. She got busier faster than she expected, and she offered me a job. Since I waited tables one summer between college semesters, I've got some experience."

He smiled. "I like it that you're helping your friend

realize her dream even though your career is stalled. That's nice."

"We grew up together. Betty was our housekeeper's daughter. When we got older my mother kept hoping I'd outgrow the friendship while Daddy helped Betty get a scholarship."

"I like that you're generous and loyal." He hesitated. "Your pictures don't do you justice. Nor did my memory of you."

His blue eyes gleamed with so much appreciation her cheeks heated. "Maybe because the last time I saw you I was slathered in mud."

He smiled. "Still, being a waitress seems like a strange job for a museum curator, even if it's temporary. You did major in art history at Princeton and completed that internship at the Metropolitan Museum of Art. I believe you graduated with honors."

She had no idea how she'd done so well, but when her grades had thrilled her father, she'd worked even harder.

"Has Daddy, who by the way, has a bad habit of talking too much, told you my life history?"

For a long moment, Quinn didn't confirm her accusation or deny it.

"Well, is that where you learned these details?"

"If he talked about you, it was because I was curious and asked him."

Not good. She frowned as she imagined her parents complaining about her disappointments since Princeton during all those family dinners she'd avoided.

"Did my father tell you that I've had a hard time with a couple of museum directors because they micromanaged me?"

"Not exactly."

"I'll bet. He takes the boss's side because he's every bit

as high-handed and dictatorial. Unfortunately, one night after finishing the setup of a new show, when I was dead tired, the director started second-guessing my judgment about stuff he'd already signed off on. I made the mistake of telling him what I really thought. When there were budget cuts, you can probably guess who he let go."

"I'm sorry about that."

"I'm good at what I do. I'll find another job, but until I do, I don't see why I shouldn't help Betty. Unfortunately, my father disagrees. We frequently disagree."

"It's your life, not his."

Her thoughts exactly. Having him concur was really sort of annoying, since Quinn was supposed to be the enemy.

In the conversational lull, she noticed that his spectacular physique was elegantly clad in a dark gray suit cut to emphasize every hard sinew of his powerful body. Suddenly, she wished she'd dressed up. Then she caught herself. Why should she care about looking her best for a man she should hate, when her appearance was something she rarely thought about?

All she'd done today was scoop her long, dark hair into a ponytail that cascaded down her back. Still, when his eyes hungrily skimmed her figure, she was glad that she'd worn the loosely flowing white shirt and long red scarf over her tight jeans because the swirls of cloth hid her body.

His burning gaze, which had ignited way too many feminine hormones, rose to her face again. When he smiled as he continued to stare, she bit her bottom lip to keep from returning his smile.

Rising, he towered over her, making her feel small and feminine and lovely in ways she'd never felt lovely before. He moved toward her, seized her hand in his much larger one and shook it gently.

"I'm very glad you decided to give me a second chance."

Why did his blunt fingers have to feel so warm and hard, his touch and gaze so deliciously intimate? She snatched her hand away, causing his eyes to flash with that pain he didn't want her to see.

"That's not what this is."

"But you *were* avoiding me, weren't you?"

"I *was*," she admitted and then instantly regretted being so truthful.

"That was a mistake—for both of us."

When he asked her if she wanted coffee or a soda or anything at all to drink, she said no and looked out the windows at the sun sinking low against the San Antonio skyline. She couldn't risk looking at him any more than necessary because her attraction seemed to be building. He would probably sense it and use it against her somehow.

With some difficulty she reminded herself that she disliked him. So, why did she still feel hot and clammy and slightly breathless, as if there were a lack of oxygen in the room?

It's called chemistry. Sexual attraction. It's irrational.

Her awareness only sharpened when he pulled out a chair for her and returned to his own. Sitting down and crossing one long leg over the other, he leaned back again. The pose should have seemed relaxed, but as he concentrated on her she could see he wasn't relaxed—he was intently assessing her.

The elegant office became eerily silent as he stared. Behind the closed doors, she felt trapped. Leaning forward, her posture grew as rigid as his was seemingly careless.

His hard, blue eyes held her motionless.

"So, to what do I owe the pleasure of your visit this afternoon...or should I say this evening?" he asked in that pleasant tone that made her tremble with excitement.

She imagined them on his megayacht, sailing silently across the vast, blue Gulf of Mexico. Her auburn hair would blow in the wind as he pulled her close and suggested they go below.

"You're my last appointment, so I can give you as much time as you want," he said, thankfully interrupting her seduction fantasy.

Her guilty heart sped up. Why had she come at such a late hour when he might not have another appointment afterward?

The sky was rapidly darkening, casting a shadow across his carved face, making him look stark and feral, adding to the danger she felt upon finding herself alone with him.

Even though her fear made her want to flee, she was far too determined to do what she had to do to give in to it.

She blurted out, "I don't want you to marry Jaycee." Oh, dear, she'd meant to lead up to this in some clever way.

He brought his blunt fingertips together in a position of prayer. When he leaned across his desk toward her, she sank lower in her own chair. "Don't you? How very strange."

"It's not strange. You can't marry her. You don't love her. You and she are too different to care for each other as a man and wife should."

His eyes darkened in a way that made him seem more alive than any man she'd ever known. "I wasn't referring to Jacinda. I was talking about you...and me and how strange that I should feel...so much—" He stopped. "When for all practical purposes we just met."

His eyes bored into hers with that piercing intensity that left her breathless. Once again she felt connected to him by some dark, forbidden, primal force.

"I never anticipated this wrinkle when I suggested a marriage with a Murray daughter," he murmured.

When his eyes slid over her body again in that devouring way, her heart raced. Her tall, slim figure wasn't appealing to most men. She'd come to believe there was nothing special about her. Could he possibly be as attracted to her as she was to him?

"You don't love her," she repeated even more shakily.

"Love? No. I don't love her. How could I? I barely know her."

"You see!"

"Your father chose her, and she agreed."

"Because she's always done everything he tells her to."

"You, however, would not have agreed so easily?" He paused. "Love does not matter to me in the least. But now I find myself curious about his choice of brides. And…even more curious about you. I want to get to know you better." His tone remained disturbingly intimate.

She remembered his revolving bedroom door and the parade of voluptuous blondes who'd passed through it. Was he so base he'd think it nothing to seduce his future wife's sister and then discard her, too?

"You've made no secret of how you feel about my father," she whispered with growing wariness. "Why marry his daughter?"

"Business. There are all these rumors in the press that I want to destroy Murray Oil, a company that once belonged to my beloved father."

"It makes perfect sense."

"No, it doesn't. I would never pay an immense amount of money for a valuable property in order to destroy it."

"But you think my father blackened your father's name and then profited after buying your father out. That's why you're so determined to destroy everything he's built, everything he loves...including Jaycee."

His lips thinned. Suddenly, his eyes were arctic. "My father built Murray Oil, not yours. Only back then it was called Sullivan and Murray Oil. Your father seized the opportunity, when my dad was down, to buy him out at five cents on the dollar."

"My father made the company what it is today."

"Well, now I'm going to take it over and improve upon it. Marriage to a Murray daughter will reassure the numerous employees that family, not a vengeful marauder, will be at the helm of the business."

"That would be a lie. You are a marauder, and you're not family."

"Not yet," he amended. "But a few Saturdays hence, if I marry Jaycee, we will be...family."

"Never. Not over my dead body!" She expelled the words in an outraged gasp.

"The thought of anything so awful happening to your delectable body is hateful to me." When he hesitated, his avid, searching expression made her warm again.

"Okay," he said. "Let's say I take you at your word. You're here to save your sister from me. And you'd die before you'd let me marry her. Is that right?"

"Essentially."

"What else would you do to stop me? Surely there is some lesser, more appealing sacrifice you'd be willing to make to inspire me to change my mind."

"I...don't know what you mean."

"Well, what if I were to agree to your proposal and forgo marriage to your lovely sister, a woman you say is so unsuited to my temperament I could never love her—I want to know what I will get in return."

"Do you always have to get something in return? You wouldn't actually be making a sacrifice."

His smile was a triumphant flash of white against his deeply tanned skin. "Always. Most decidedly. My hypothetical marriage to your sister is a business deal, after all. As a businessman, I would require compensation for letting the deal fall through."

Awful man.

His blue eyes stung her, causing the pulse in her throat to hammer frantically.

"Maybe...er...the satisfaction of doing a good deed for once in your life?" she said.

He laughed. "That's a refreshing idea if ever I heard one, and from a very charming woman—but, like most humans, I'm driven by the desire to avoid pain and pursue pleasure."

"And to think—I imagined you to be primarily driven by greed. Well, I don't have any money."

"I don't want your money."

"What do you want, then?"

"I think you know," he said silkily, leaning closer. "*You. You* interest me...quite a lot. I believe we could give each other immense pleasure...under the right circumstances."

The unavoidable heat in his eyes caused an unwanted shock wave of fiery prickles to spread through her body. She'd seriously underestimated the risk of confronting this man.

"In fact, I think we both knew what we wanted the moment we looked at each other today," he said.

He wanted her.

And even though he was promised to Jaycee, he didn't have a qualm about acknowledging his impossible, unsavory need for the skinnier, plainer, older sister. Maybe the thought of bedding his future wife's sister improved upon his original idea of revenge. Or maybe he was simply a man who never denied himself a female who might amuse him, however briefly. If any of those assumptions were true, he was too horrible for words.

"I'm hungry," he continued. "Why don't we discuss your proposition over dinner," he said.

"No. I couldn't possibly. You've said more than enough to convince me of the kind of man you are."

"Who are you kidding? You were prejudiced against me before you showed up here. If I'd played the saint, you would have still thought me the devil…and yet you would have also still…been secretly attracted. And you are attracted to me. Admit it."

Stunned at his boldness, she hissed out a breath. "I'm not."

Then why was she staring at his darling dimple as if she was hypnotized by it?

He laughed. "Do you have a boyfriend?" he asked. "Or dinner plans you need to change?"

"No," she admitted before she thought.

"Good." He smiled at her as if he was genuinely pleased. "Then it's settled."

"What?"

"You and I have a dinner date."

"No!"

"What are you afraid of?" he asked in that deep, velvet tone that let her know he had much more than dinner in mind. And some part of her, God help her, wanted to rush toward him like a moth toward flame, despite her sister, despite the knowledge that he wanted to destroy her family.

Kira was shaking her head vehemently when he said, "You came here today to talk to me, to convince me to do as you ask. I'm making myself available to you."

"But?"

He gave her a slow, insolent grin. "If you want to save your sister from the Big Bad Wolf, well—here's your chance."

Two

When they turned the corner and she saw the gaily lit restaurant, Kira wished with all her heart she'd never agreed to this dinner with Quinn.

Not that he hadn't behaved like a perfect gentleman as they'd walked over together.

When she'd said she wanted to go somewhere within walking distance of his office, she'd foolishly thought she'd be safer with him on foot.

"You're not afraid to get in my car, to be alone with me, are you?" he'd teased.

"It just seems simpler…to go somewhere close," she'd hedged. "Besides, you're a busy man."

"Not too busy for what really matters."

Then he'd suggested they walk along the river. The lovely reflections in the still, brown water where ducks swam and the companionable silences they'd shared as they'd made their way along the flagstones edged by lush vegetation, restaurants and bars had been altogether too enjoyable.

She'd never made a study of predators, but she had a cat, Rudy. When on the hunt, he was purposeful, diligent and very patient. He enjoyed playing with his prey before the kill, just to make the game last longer. She couldn't help but think Quinn was doing something similar with her.

No sooner did Quinn push open the door so she could enter one of the most popular Mexican restaurants in all of San Antonio than warmth, vibrant laughter and the heavy beat of Latin music hit her.

A man, who was hurrying outside after a woman, said, "Oh, excuse us, please, miss."

Quinn reached out and put his strong arm protectively around Kira's waist, shielding her with his powerful body. Pulling her close, he tugged her to one side to let the other couple pass.

When Quinn's body brushed against hers intimately, as if they were a couple, heat washed over her as it had the afternoon when she'd been muddy and he'd pulled her into his arms. She inhaled his clean, male scent. As before, he drew her like a sexual magnet.

When she let out an excited little gasp, he smiled and pulled her even closer. "You feel much too good," he whispered.

She should run, but the March evening was cooler than she'd dressed for, causing her to instinctively cling to his hot, big-boned body and stay nestled against his welcoming warmth.

She felt the red scarf she wore around her neck tighten as if to warn her away. She yanked at it and gulped in a breath before she shoved herself free of him.

He laughed. "You're not the only one who's been stunned by our connection, you know. I like holding you as much as you like being in my arms. In fact, that's all I want to do…hold you. Does that make me evil? Or all too human because I've found a woman I have no will to resist?"

"You are too much! Why did I let you talk me into this dinner?"

"Because it was the logical thing to do, and I insisted. Because I'm very good at getting what I want. Maybe because *you* wanted to. But now I'd be quite happy to skip dinner. We could order takeout and go to my loft apartment, which isn't far, by the way. You're a curator. I'm a collector. I have several pieces that might interest you."

"I'll bet! Not a good idea."

Again he laughed.

She didn't feel any safer once they were inside the crowded, brilliantly lit establishment. The restaurant with its friendly waitstaff, strolling mariachis, delicious aromas and ceiling festooned with tiny lights and colorful banners was too festive, too conducive to lowering one's guard. It would be too easy to succumb to temptation, something she couldn't afford to do.

I'll have a taco, a glass of water. We'll talk about Jaycee, and I'll leave. What could possibly go wrong if I nip this attraction in the bud?

When told there was a thirty-minute wait, Quinn didn't seem to mind. To the contrary, he seemed pleased. "We'll wait in the bar," he said, smiling.

Then he ushered them into a large room with a high-beamed ceiling dominated by a towering carved oak bar, inspired by the baroque elegance of the hotels in nineteenth-century San Antonio.

When a young redheaded waiter bragged on the various imported tequilas available, Quinn ordered them two margaritas made of a particularly costly tequila he said he had a weakness for.

"I'd rather have sparkling water," she said, sitting up straighter, thinking she needed all her wits about her.

"As you wish," Quinn said gallantly, ordering the water as well, but she noted that he didn't cancel the second margarita.

When their drinks arrived, he lifted his margarita to his lips and licked at the salt that edged the rim. And just watching the movement of his tongue across the grit of those glimmering crystals flooded her with ridiculous heat as she imagined him licking her skin.

"I think our first dinner together calls for a toast, don't you?" he said.

Her hand moved toward her glass of sparkling water.

"The tequila really is worth a taste."

She looked into his eyes and hesitated. Almost without her knowing it, her hand moved slowly away from the icy glass of water to her chilled margarita glass.

"You won't be sorry," he promised in that silken baritone.

Toying with the slender green stem of her glass, she lifted it and then tentatively clinked it against his.

"To us," he said. "To new beginnings." He smiled benevolently, but his blue eyes were excessively brilliant.

Her first swallow of the margarita was salty, sweet and very strong. She knew she shouldn't drink any more. Then, almost at once, a pleasant warmth buzzed through her, softening her attitude toward him and weakening her willpower. Somewhere the mariachis began to play "La Paloma," a favorite love song of hers. Was it a sign?

"I'm glad you at least took a sip," he said, his gaze lingering on her lips a second too long. "It would be a pity to miss tasting something so delicious."

"You're right. It's really quite good."

"The best—all the more reason not to miss it. One can't retrace one's journey in this life. We must make the most of every moment…because once lost, those moments are gone forever."

"Indeed." Eyeing him, she sipped again. "Funny, I hadn't thought of you as a philosopher."

"You might be surprised by who I really am, if you took the trouble to get to know me."

"I doubt it."

Every muscle in his handsome face tensed. When his eyes darkened, she wondered if she'd wounded him.

No. Impossible.

Her nerves jingled, urging her to consider just one more sip of the truly delicious margarita. What could it hurt? That second sip led to a third, then another and another, each sliding down her throat more easily than the last. She hardly noticed when Quinn moved from his side of the booth to hers, and yet how could she not notice? He didn't touch her, yet it was thrilling to be so near him, to know that only their clothes separated her thigh from his, to wonder what he would do next.

His gaze never strayed from her. Focusing on her exclusively, he told her stories about his youth, about the time before his father had died. His father had played ball with him, he said, had taken him hunting and fishing, had helped him with his homework. He stayed off the grim subjects of his parents' divorce and his father's death.

"When school was out for any reason, he always took me to his office. He was determined to instill a work ethic in me."

"He sounds like the perfect father," she said wistfully. "I never seemed to be able to please mine. If he read to me, I fidgeted too much, and he would lose his place and his temper. If he took me fishing, I grew bored or hot and squirmed too much, kicking over the minnow bucket or snapping his line. Once I stood up too fast and turned the boat over."

"Maybe I won't take you fishing."

"He always wanted a son, and I didn't please Mother any better. She thought Jaycee, who loved to dress up and go to parties, was perfect. She still does. Neither of them like what I'm doing with my life."

"Well, they're not in control, are they? No one is, really. And just when we think we are, we usually get struck by a lightning bolt that shows us we're not," Quinn said in a silken tone that made her breath quicken. "Like tonight."

"What do you mean?"

"Us."

Her gaze fixed on his dimple. "Are you coming on to me?"

He laid his hand on top of hers. "Would that be so terrible?"

By the time they'd been seated at their dinner table and had ordered their meal, she'd lost all her fear of him. She was actually enjoying herself.

Usually, she dated guys who couldn't afford to take her out to eat very often, so she cooked for them in her apartment. Even though this meal was not a date, it was nice to dine in a pleasant restaurant and be served for a change.

When Quinn said how sorry he was that they hadn't met before that afternoon when he'd nearly run her down, she answered truthfully, "I thought you were marrying my sister solely to hurt all of us. I couldn't condone that."

He frowned. "And you love your sister so much, you came to my office today to try to find a way to stop me from marrying her."

"I was a fool to admit that to you."

"I think you're sweet, and I admire your honesty. You were right to come. You did me one helluva favor. I've been on the wrong course. But I don't want to talk about Jacinda. I want to talk about you."

"But will you think about…not marrying her?"

When he nodded and said, "Definitely," in a very convincing manner, she relaxed and took still another sip of her margarita with no more thoughts of how dangerous it might be for her to continue relaxing around him.

When he reached across the table and wrapped her hand in his warm, blunt fingers, the shock of his touch sent a wave of heat through her whole body. For a second, she entwined her fingers with his and clung as if he were a vital lifeline. Then, when she realized what she was doing, she wrenched her hand free.

"Why are you so afraid of me, Kira?"

"You might still marry Jaycee and ruin her life," she lied.

"Impossible, now that I've met you."

Kira's breath quickened. Dimple or not, he was still the enemy. She had to remember that.

"Do you really think I'm so callous I could marry your sister when I want you so much?"

"But what are you going to do about Jaycee?"

"I told you. She became irrelevant the minute I saw you standing inside my office this afternoon."

"She's beautiful…and *blonde.*"

"Yes, but your beauty affects me more. Don't you know that?"

She shook her head. "The truth isn't in you. You only date blondes."

"Then it must be time for a change."

"I'm going to confess a secret wish. All my life I wished I was blonde…so I'd look more like the rest of my family, especially my mother and my sister. I thought maybe then I'd feel like I belonged."

"You *are* beautiful."

"A man like you would say anything…"

"I've never lied to any woman. Don't you know how incredibly lovely you are? With your shining dark eyes that show your sweet, pure soul every time you look at me and defend your sister? I feel your love for her rushing through you like liquid electricity. You're graceful. You move like a ballerina. I love the way you feel so intensely and blush when you think I might touch you."

"Like a child."

"No. Like a responsive, passionate woman. I like that… too much. And your hair…it's long and soft and shines like chestnut satin. Yet there's fire in it. I want to run my hands through it."

"But we hardly know one another. And I've hated you…"

"None of the Murrays have been favorites of mine either…but I'm beginning to see the error of my ways. And I don't think you hate me as much as you pretend."

Kira stared at him, searching his hard face for some sign that he was lying to her, seducing her as he'd seduced all those other women, saying these things because he had some dark agenda. All she saw was warmth and honesty and intense emotion. Nobody had ever looked at her with such hunger or made her feel so beautiful.

All her life she'd wanted someone to make her feel this special. It was ironic that Quinn Sullivan should be the one.

"I thought you were so bad, no…pure evil," she repeated.

His eyebrows arched. "Ouch."

If he'd been twisted in his original motives, maybe it

had been because of the grief he'd felt at losing someone he loved.

"How could I have been so wrong about you?" Even as she said it, some part of her wondered if she weren't being naive. He had dated, and jilted, all those beautiful women. He had intended to take revenge on her father and use her sister in his plan. Maybe when she'd walked into his office she'd become part of his diabolical plan, too.

"I was misguided," he said.

"I need more time to think about all this. Like I said…a mere hour or two ago I heartily disliked you. Or at least I thought I did."

"Because you didn't know me. Hell, maybe I didn't know me either…because everything is different now, since I met you."

She felt the same way. But she knew she should slow it down, reassess.

"I'm not good at picking boyfriends," she whispered.

"Their loss."

His hand closed over hers and he pressed her fingers, causing a melting sensation in her tummy. "My gain."

Her tacos came, looking and smelling delicious, but she hardly touched them. Her every sense was attuned to Quinn's carved features and his beautiful voice.

When a musician came to their table, Quinn hired him to sing several songs, including "La Paloma." While the man serenaded her, Quinn idly stroked her wrist and the length of her fingers, causing fire to shoot down her spine.

She met his eyes and felt that she had known him always, that he was already her lover, her soul mate. She was crazy to feel such things and think such thoughts about a man she barely knew, but when dinner was over, they skipped dessert.

An hour later, she sat across from him in his downtown

loft, sipping coffee while he drank brandy. In vain, she tried to act unimpressed by his art collection and sparkling views of the city. Not easy, since both were impressive.

His entrance was filled with an installation of crimson light by one of her favorite artists. The foyer was a dazzling ruby void that opened into a living room with high, white ceilings. All the rooms of his apartment held an eclectic mix of sculpture, porcelains and paintings.

Although she hadn't yet complimented his stylish home, she couldn't help but compare her small, littered apartment to his spacious one. Who was she to label him an arrogant upstart? He was a success in the international oil business and a man of impeccable taste, while she was still floundering in her career and struggling to find herself.

"I wanted to be alone with you like this the minute I saw you today," he said.

She shifted uneasily on his cream-leather sofa. Yet more evidence that he was a planner. "Well, I didn't."

"I think you did. You just couldn't let yourself believe you did."

"No," she whispered, setting down her cup. With difficulty she tried to focus on her mission. "So, what about Jaycee? You're sure that's over?"

"Finished. From the first moment I saw you."

"Without mud all over my face."

He laughed. "Actually, you got to me that day, too. Every time I dined with Jacinda and your family, I kept hoping I'd meet you again."

Even as she remembered all those dinner invitations her parents had extended and she'd declined, she couldn't believe he was telling the truth.

"I had my team research you," he said.

"Why?"

"I asked myself the same question. I think you intrigued

me...like I said, even with mud on your face. First thing tomorrow, I will break it off with Jacinda formally. Which means you've won. Does that make you happy? You have what you came for."

He was all charm, especially his warm, white smile. Like a child with a new playmate, she was happy just being with him, but she couldn't admit that to him.

He must have sensed her feelings, though, because he got up and moved silently toward her. "I feel like I've lived my whole life since my father's death alone—until you. And that's how I wanted to live—until you."

She knew it was sudden and reckless, but she felt the same way. If she wasn't careful, she would forget all that should divide them.

As if in a dream, she took his hand when he offered it and kissed his fingers with feverish devotion.

"You've made me realize how lonely I've been," he said.

"That's a very good line."

"It's the truth."

"But you are so successful, while I..."

"Look what you're doing in the interim—helping a friend to realize her dream."

"My father says I'm wasting my potential."

"You will find yourself...if you are patient." He cupped her chin and stared into her eyes. Again she felt that uncanny recognition. He was a kindred soul who knew what it was to feel lost.

"Dear God," he muttered. "Don't listen to me. I don't know a damn thing about patience. Like now... I should let you go...but I can't."

He pulled her to him and crushed her close. It wasn't long before holding her wasn't enough. He had to have her lips, her throat, her breasts. She felt the same way. Shedding her shirt, scarf and bra, she burst into flame as he kissed her. Even though she barely knew him, she could not wait another moment to belong to him.

"I'm not feeling so patient right now myself," she admitted huskily.

Do not give yourself to this man, said an inner voice. *Remember all those blondes. Remember his urge for revenge.*

Even as her emotions spiraled out of control, she knew she was no femme fatale, while he was a devastatingly attractive man. Had he said all these same wonderful things to all those other women he'd bedded? Had he done and felt all the same things, too, a thousand times before? Were nights like this routine for him, while he was the first to make her feel so thrillingly alive?

But then his mouth claimed hers again, and again, with a fierce, wild hunger that made her forget her doubts and shake and cling to him. His kisses completed her as she'd never been completed before. He was a wounded soul, and she understood his wounds. How could she feel so much when they hadn't even made love?

Lifting her into his arms, he carried her into his vast bedroom, which was bathed in silver moonlight. Over her shoulder she saw his big, black bed in the middle of an ocean of white marble and Persian carpets.

He was a driven, successful billionaire, and she was a waitress. Feeling out of her depth, her nerves returned. Not knowing what else to do, she pressed a fingertip to his lips. Gently, shyly, she traced his dimple.

Feeling her tension, he set her down. She pushed against his chest and then took a step away from him. Watching her, he said, "You can finish undressing in the bathroom if you'd prefer privacy. Or we can stop. I'll drive you to your car. Your choice."

She should have said, "I don't belong here with you,"

and accepted his gallant offer. Instead, without a word, she scampered toward the door he'd indicated. Alone in his beige marble bathroom with golden fixtures and a lovely, compelling etching by another one of her favorite artists, she barely recognized her own flushed face, tousled hair and sparkling eyes.

The radiant girl in his tall mirror *was* as beautiful as an enchanted princess. She looked expectant, excited. Maybe she did belong here with him. Maybe he was the beginning of her new life, the first correct step toward the bright future that had so long eluded her.

When she tiptoed back into the bedroom, wearing nothing but his white robe, he was in bed. She couldn't help admiring the width of his bronzed shoulders as he leaned back against several plumped pillows. She had never dated anyone half so handsome; she'd never felt anything as powerful as the glorious heady heat that suffused her entire being as his blue eyes studied her hungrily. Still, she was nervy, shaking.

"I'm no good at sex," she said. "You're probably very good... Of course you are. You're good at everything."

"Come here," he whispered.

"But..."

"Just come to me. You could not possibly delight me more. Surely you know that."

Did he really feel as much as she did?

Removing his bathrobe, she flew to him before she lost her nerve, fell into his bed and into his arms, consumed by forces beyond her control. Nothing mattered but sliding against his long body, being held close in his strong arms. Beneath the covers, his heat was delicious and welcoming as she nestled against him.

He gave her a moment to settle before he rolled on top of her. Bracing himself with his elbows against the mattress, so as not to crush her, he kissed her lips, her cheeks, her brows and then her eyelids with urgent yet featherlike strokes. Slowly, gently, each kiss was driving her mad.

"Take me," she whispered, in the grip of a fever such as she'd never experienced before. "I want you inside me. Now."

"I know," he said, laughing. "I'm as ravenous as you are. But have patience, darlin'."

"You have a funny way of showing your hunger."

"If I do what you ask, it would be over in a heartbeat. This moment, our first time together, is too special to me."

Was she special?

"We must savor it, draw it out, make it last," he said.

"Maybe I want it to be over swiftly," she begged. "Maybe this obsessive need is unbearable."

"Exquisite expectation?"

"I can't stand it."

"And I want to heighten it. Which means we're at cross-purposes."

He didn't take her. With infinite care and maddening patience he adored her with his clever mouth and skilled hands. His fevered lips skimmed across her soft skin, raising goose bumps in secret places. As she lay beneath him, he licked each nipple until it grew hard, licked her navel until he had all her nerve endings on fire for him. Then he kissed her belly and dived even lower to explore those hidden, honey-sweet lips between her legs. When she felt his tongue dart inside, she gasped and drew back.

"Relax," he whispered.

With slow, hot kisses, he made her gush. All too soon her embarrassment was gone, and she was melting, shivering, whimpering—all but begging him to give her release.

Until tonight she had been an exile in the world of love. With all other men, not that there had been that many, she had been going through the motions, playing a part, searching always for something meaningful and never finding it.

Until now, tonight, with him.

He couldn't matter this much! She couldn't let this be more than fierce, wild sex. He, the man, couldn't matter. But her building emotions told her that he did matter—in ways she'd never imagined possible before.

He took her breast in his mouth and suckled again. Then his hand entered her heated wetness, making her gasp helplessly and plead. When he stroked her, his fingers sliding against that secret flesh, she arched against his expert touch, while her breath came in hard, tortured pants.

Just when she didn't think she could bear it any longer, he dragged her beneath him and slid inside her. He was huge, massive, wonderful. Crying out, she clung to him and pushed her pelvis against his, aching for him to fill her even more deeply. *"Yes! Yes!"*

When he sank deeper, ever deeper, she moaned. For a long moment he held her and caressed her. Then he began to plunge in and out, slowly at first. Her rising pleasure carried her and shook her in sharp, hot waves, causing her to climax and scream his name.

He went crazy when she dug her nails in his shoulder. Then she came again, and again, sobbing. She had no idea how many climaxes she had before she felt his hard loins bunch as he exploded.

Afterward, sweat dripped off his brow. His whole body was flushed, burning up, and so was hers.

"Darlin' Kira," he whispered in that husky baritone that could still make her shiver even when she was spent. "Darlin' Kira."

For a long time, she lay in his arms, not speaking, feeling too weak to move any part of her body. Then he leaned over and nibbled at her bottom lip.

The second time he made love to her, he did so with a reverent gentleness that made her weep and hold on to him for a long time afterward. He'd used a condom the second time, causing her to realize belatedly that he hadn't the first time.

How could they have been so careless? She had simply been swept away. Maybe he had, too. Well, it was useless to worry about that now. Besides, she was too happy, too relaxed to care about anything except being in his arms. There was no going back.

For a long time they lay together, facing each other while they talked. He told her about his father's financial crisis and how her father had turned on him and made things worse. He spoke of his mother's extravagance and betrayal and his profound hurt that his world had fallen apart so quickly and brutally. She listened as he explained how grief, poverty and helplessness had twisted him and made him hard.

"Love made me too vulnerable, as it did my father. It was a destructive force. My father loved my mother, and it ruined him. She was greedy and extravagant," he said. "Love destroys the men in our family."

"If you don't want to love, why did you date all those women I read about?"

"I wasn't looking for love, and neither were they."

"You were just using them, then?"

"They were using me, too."

"That's so cynical."

"That's how my life has been. I loved my father so much, and I hurt so much when he died, I gave up on love. He loved my mother, and she broke his heart with her unrelenting demands. When he lost the business, she lost interest in him and began searching for a richer man."

"And did she find him?"

"Several."

"Do you ever see her?"

"No. I was an accident she regretted, I believe. She couldn't relate to children, and after I was grown, I had no interest in her. Love, no matter what kind, always costs too much. I do write her a monthly check, however."

"So, my father was only part of your father's problem."

"But a big part. Losing ownership in Sullivan and Murray Oil made my father feel like he was less than nothing. My mother left him because of that loss. She stripped him of what little wealth and self-esteem he had left. Alone, without his company or his wife, he grew depressed. He wouldn't eat. He couldn't sleep. I'd hear the stairs creak as he paced at night.

"Then early one morning I heard a shot. When I called his name, he didn't answer. I found him in the shop attached to our garage. In a pool of blood on the floor, dead. I still don't know if it was an accident or...what I feared it was. He was gone. At first I was frightened. Then I became angry. I wanted to blame someone, to get even, to make his death right. I lived for revenge. But now that I've almost achieved my goal of taking back Murray Oil, it's as if my fever's burned out."

"Oh, I wouldn't say that," she teased, touching his damp brow.

"I mean my fever for revenge, which was what kept me going."

"So," she asked, "what will you live for now?"

"I don't know. I guess a lot of people just wake up in the morning and go to work, then come home at night and drink while they flip channels with their remote."

"Not you."

"Who's to say? Maybe such people are lucky. At least they're not driven by hate, as I was."

"I can't even begin to imagine what that must have felt like for you." She'd always been driven by the need for love.

When he stared into her eyes with fierce longing, she pulled him close and ran her hands through his hair. "You are young yet. You'll find something to give your life meaning," she said.

"Well, it won't be love, because I've experienced love's dark side for too many years. I want you to know that. You are special, but I can't ever love you, no matter how good we are together. I'm no longer capable of that emotion."

"So you keep telling me," she said, pretending his words didn't hurt.

"I just want to be honest."

"Do we always know our own truths?"

"Darlin'," he whispered. "Forgive me if I sounded too harsh. It's just that…I don't want to hurt you by raising your expectations about something I'm incapable of. Other women have become unhappy because of the way I am."

"You're my family's enemy. Why would I ever want to love you?"

Wrapping her legs around him, she held him for hours, trying to comfort the boy who'd lost so much as well as the angry man who'd gained a fortune because he'd been consumed by a fierce, if misplaced, hatred.

"My father had nothing to do with your father's death," she whispered. "He didn't."

"You have your view, and I have mine," he said. "The important thing is that I don't hold you responsible for your father's sins any longer."

"Don't you?"

"No."

After that, he was silent. Soon afterward he let her go and rolled onto his side.

She lay awake for hours. Where would they go from here? He had hated her family for years. Had he really let go of all those harsh feelings? Had she deluded herself into thinking he wasn't her enemy?

What price would she pay for sleeping with a man who probably only saw her as an instrument for revenge?

Three

When Kira woke up naked in bed with Quinn, she felt unsettled and very self-conscious. Propping herself on an elbow, she watched him warily in the dim rosy half light of dawn. All her doubts returned a hundredfold.

How could she have let things go this far? How could she have risked pregnancy?

What if… No, she couldn't be that unlucky.

Besides, it did no good to regret what had happened, she reminded herself again. If she hadn't slept with him she would never have known such ecstasy was possible.

Now, at least, she knew. Even if it wasn't love, it had been so great she felt an immense tenderness well up in her in spite of her renewed doubts.

He was absurdly handsome with his thick, unruly black hair falling across his brow, with his sharp cheekbones and sculpted mouth. She'd been touched when he'd shown her his vulnerability last night. Just looking at him now was enough to make her stomach flutter with fresh desire.

She was about to stroke his hair, when, without warning, his obscenely long lashes snapped open, and he met her gaze with that directness that still startled her. Maybe because there were so many imperfections she wanted to keep hidden. In the next instant, his expression softened, disarming her.

"Good morning, darlin'." His rough, to-die-for, sexy baritone caressed her.

A jolt sizzled through her even before he reached out a bronzed hand to pull her face to his so he could kiss her lightly on the lips. Never had she wanted anyone as much as she wanted him.

"I haven't brushed my teeth," she warned.

"Neither the hell have I. I don't expect you to be perfect. I simply want you. I can't do without you. You should know that after last night."

She was amazed because she felt exactly the same. Still, with those doubts still lingering, she felt she had to protect herself by protesting.

"Last night was probably a mistake," she murmured.

"Maybe. Or maybe it's a complication, a challenge. Or a good thing. In any case, it's too late to worry about it. I want you more now than ever."

"But for how long?"

"Is anything certain?"

He kissed her hard. Before she could protest again, he rolled on top of her and was inside her, claiming her fiercely, his body piercing her to the bed, his massive erection filling her. When he rode her violently, she bucked like a wild thing, too, her doubts dissolving like mist as primal desire swept her past reason.

"I'm sorry," he said afterward. "I wanted you too much."

He had, however, at the last second, remembered to use a condom. This time, he didn't hold her tenderly or make small talk or confide sweet nothings as he had last night. In fact, he seemed hellishly annoyed at himself.

Was he already tired of her? Would there be a new blonde in his bed tonight? At the thought, a sob caught in her throat.

"You can have the master bathroom. I'll make coffee," he said tersely.

Just like that, he wanted her gone. Since she'd researched him and had known his habits, she shouldn't feel shocked or hurt. Hadn't he warned her he was incapable of feeling close to anyone? She should be grateful for the sublime sexual experience and let the rest go.

Well, she had her pride. She wasn't about to cling to him or show that she cared. But she did care. Oh, how she cared. Her family's worst enemy had quickly gained a curious hold on her heart.

Without a word, she rose and walked naked across the vast expanse of thick, white carpet, every female cell vividly aware that, bored with her though he might be, he didn't tear his eyes from her until she reached the bathroom and shut the door. Once inside she turned the lock and leaned heavily against the wall in a state of collapse.

She took a deep breath and stared at her pale, guilt-stricken reflection, so different from the glowing wanton of last night.

She'd known the kind of guy he was, in spite of his seductive words. How could she have opened herself to such a hard man? Her father's implacable enemy?

What had she done?

By the time she'd showered, brushed her hair and dressed, he was in the kitchen, looking no worse for wear.

Indeed, he seemed energized by what they had shared. Freshly showered, he wore a white shirt and crisply pressed dark slacks. He'd shaved, and his glossy black hair was combed. He looked so civilized, she felt the crazy urge to run her hands through his hair, just to muss it up and leave her mark.

The television was on, and he was watching the latest stock market report while he held his cell phone against his ear. Behind him, a freshly made pot of aromatic coffee sat on the gleaming white counter.

She was about to step inside when he flicked the remote, killing the sound of the television. She heard his voice, as sharp and hard as it had been with the caller yesterday in his office.

"Habib, business is business," he snapped. "I know I have to convince the shareholders and the public I'm some shining white knight. That's why I agreed to marry a Murray daughter and why her parents, especially her father, who wants an easy transition of power, suggested Jacinda and persuaded her to accept me. However, if the older Murray sister agrees to marry me instead, why should it matter to you or to anyone else…other than to Jacinda, who will no doubt be delighted to have her life back?"

Habib, whoever he was, must have argued, because Quinn's next response was much angrier. "Yes, I know the family history and why you consider Jacinda the preferable choice, but since nobody else knows, apparently not even Kira, it's of no consequence. So, if I've decided to marry the older sister instead of the younger, and this decision will make the shareholders and employees just as happy, why the hell should you care?"

The man must have countered again, because Quinn's low tone was even more cutting. "No, I haven't asked her yet. It's too soon. But when I do, I'll remind her that I told her yesterday I'd demand a price for freeing her sister. She'll have to pay it, that's all. She'll have no choice but to do what's best for her family and her sister. Hell, she'll do anything for their approval."

One sister or the other—and he didn't care which one. That he could speak of marrying her instead of Jaycee as a cold business deal before he'd even bothered to propose made Kira's tender heart swell with hurt and outrage. That he would use her desire for her family's love and acceptance to his own advantage was too horrible to endure.

Obviously, she was that insignificant to him. But hadn't she known that? So why did it hurt so much?

He'd said she was special. Nobody had ever made her feel so cherished before.

Thinking herself a needy, romantic fool, she shut her eyes. Unready to face him or confess what she'd overheard and how much it bothered her, Kira backed out of the kitchen and returned to the bedroom. In her present state she was incapable of acting rationally and simply demanding an explanation.

He was a planner. Her seduction must have been a calculated move. No longer could she believe he'd been swept off his feet by her as she had by him. She was skinny and plain. He'd known she desired him, and he was using that to manipulate her.

Last night, when he'd promised he'd break it off with her sister, she'd never guessed the devious manner in which he'd planned to honor that promise.

She was still struggling to process everything she'd learned, when Quinn himself strode into the bedroom looking much too arrogant, masterful and self-satisfied for her liking.

"Good, you're dressed," he said in that beautiful voice. "You look gorgeous."

Refusing to meet the warmth of his admiring gaze for fear she might believe his compliment and thereby lose her determination to escape him, she nodded.

"I made coffee."

"Smells good," she whispered, staring out the window.

"Do you have time for breakfast?"

"No!"

"Something wrong?"

If he was dishonest, why should she bother to be straight with him? "I'm fine," she said, but in a softer tone.

"Right. That must be why you seem so cool."

"Indeed?"

"And they say men are the ones who withdraw the morning after."

She bit her lip to keep herself from screaming at him.

"Still, I understand," he said.

"Last night is going to take some getting used to," she said.

"For me, as well."

To that she said nothing.

"Well, the coffee's in the kitchen," he said, turning away.

Preferring to part from him without an argument, she followed him into the kitchen where he poured her a steaming cup and handed it to her.

"Do you take cream? Sugar?"

She shook her head. "We don't know the most basic things about each other, do we?"

"After last night, I'd have to disagree with you, darlin'."

She blushed in confusion. "Don't call me that."

He eyed her thoughtfully. "You really do seem upset."

She sipped from her cup, again choosing silence instead of arguing the point. Was he good at everything? Rich and strong, the coffee was to die for.

"For the record, I take mine black, very black," he said.

"Without sugar. So, we have that in common. And we have what we shared last night."

"Don't…"

"I'd say we're off to a great start."

Until I realized what you were up to, I would have agreed. She longed to claw him. Instead, she clenched her nails into her palms and chewed her lower lip mutinously.

The rosy glow from last night, when he'd made her feel so special, had faded. She felt awkward and unsure…and hurt, which was ridiculous because she'd gone into this knowing who and what he was.

Obviously, last night had been business as usual for him. Why not marry the Murray sister who'd practically thrown herself at him? Did he believe she was so smitten and desperate for affection she'd be more easily controlled?

Why had she let herself be swept away by his looks, his confidences and his suave, expert lovemaking?

Because, your stupid crush on him turned your brain to mush.

And turned her raging hormones to fire. Never had she felt so physically and spiritually in tune with anyone. She'd actually thought, at one point, that they could be soul mates.

Soul mates! It was all an illusion. You were a fool, girl, and not for the first time.

"Look, I'd really better go," she said, her tone so sharp his dark head jerked toward her.

"Right. Then I'll drive you, since you left your car downtown."

"I can call a cab."

"No! I'll drive you."

Silently, she nodded.

He led the way to stairs that went down to the elevator and garage. In silence, they sped along the freeway in his

silver Aston Martin until he slowed to take the off-ramp
that led to where she'd parked downtown. After that, she
had to speak to him in order to direct him to her small,
dusty Toyota with several dings in its beige body. She let
out a little moan when he pulled up behind her car and
she saw the parking ticket flapping under her windshield
wipers.

He got out and raced around the hood to open her door,
but before he could, she'd flung it open.

"You sure there isn't something wrong?" he asked.

She snatched the ticket, but before she could get in her
car, he slid his arms around her waist from behind.

He felt so solid and strong and warm, she barely suppressed a sigh. She yearned to stay in his arms even though
she knew she needed to get away from him as quickly as
possible to regroup.

He turned her to face him and his fingertips traced the
length of her cheek in a tender, burning caress, and for a
long second he stared into her troubled eyes with a mixture
of concern and barely suppressed impatience. He seemed
to care.

Liar.

"It's not easy letting you go," he said.

"People are watching us," she said mildly, even as she
seethed with outrage.

"So what? Last night was very special to me, Kira. I'm
sorry if you're upset about it. I hope it's just that it all happened too fast. I wasn't too rough, was I?"

The concern in his voice shook her. "No." She looked
away, too tempted to meet his gaze.

"It's never been like that for me. I…I couldn't control
myself, especially this morning. I wanted you again…
badly. This is all happening too fast for me, too. I prefer
being able to plan."

That's not what he'd said on the phone. Quinn seemed to have damn sure had a plan. Marry a Murray daughter. And he was sticking to it.

"Yes, it is happening…too fast." She bit her lip. "But… I'm okay." She wanted to brush off his words, to pretend she didn't care that he'd apologized and seemed genuinely worried about her physical and emotional state. He seemed all too likable. She almost believed him.

"Do you have a business card?" he asked gently.

She shook her head. "Nope. At least, not on me."

He flipped a card out of his pocket. "Well, here is mine. You can call me anytime. I want to see you again…as soon as possible. There's something very important I want to discuss with you."

The intensity of his gaze made her heart speed up. "You are not going back on your word about marrying Jaycee, are you?"

"How can you even ask? I'll call it off as soon as I leave you. Unfortunately, after that, I have to be away on business for several days, first to New York, then London. Murray Oil is in the middle of negotiating a big deal with the European Union. My meeting tonight in New York ends at eight, so call me after that. On my cell."

Did he intend to propose over the phone? Her throat felt thick as she forced herself to nod. Whipping out a pen and a pad, she wrote down her cell phone number. "Will you text me as soon as you break up with my sister?"

"Can I take that to mean you care about me…a little?" he asked.

"Sure," she whispered, exhaling a pent-up breath. How did he lie so easily? "Take it any way you like."

She had to get away from him, to be alone to think. Everything he said, everything he did, made her want him—even though she knew, after what she'd heard this morning, that she'd never been anything but a pawn in the game he was playing to exact revenge against her father.

She wasn't special to him. And if she didn't stand up for herself now, she never would be.

She would not let her father sell Jaycee *or* her to this man!

Four

"You're her father. I still can't believe you don't have a clue where Kira could be. Hell, she's been gone for nearly three weeks."

Shaking his head, Earl stalked across Quinn's corner office at Murray Oil to look out the window. "I told you, she's probably off somewhere painting. She does that."

Quinn hated himself for having practically ordered the infuriating Murray to his office again today. But he was that desperate to know Kira was safe. Her safety aside, he had a wedding planned and a bride to locate.

"You're sure she's not in any trouble?"

"Are *you* sure she didn't realize you were about to demand that she marry you?"

Other than wanting Kira to take Jaycee's place, he wasn't sure about a damn thing! Well, except that maybe he'd pushed Kira too fast and too far. Hell, she could have overheard him talking to Habib. She'd damn sure gotten quiet and sulky before they parted ways.

"I don't think—"

"I'd bet money she got wise to you and decided to let you stew in your own juices. She may seem sweet and malleable, but she's always had a mind of her own. She's impossible to control. It's why she lost her job. It's why I suggested you choose Jaycee in the first place. Jaycee is biddable."

Quinn felt heat climb his neck. He didn't want Jaycee. He'd never wanted Jaycee. He wanted Kira...sweet, passionate Kira who went wild every time he touched her. Her passion thrilled him as nothing else had in years.

The trouble was, after he'd made love to her that morning, he'd felt completely besotted and then out of sorts as a result. He hadn't wanted to dwell on what feeling such an all-consuming attraction so quickly might mean. Now he knew that if anything had happened to her, he'd never forgive himself.

"I couldn't ask her to marry me after our dinner. It was too soon. Hell, maybe she did figure it all out and run off before I could explain."

"Well, I checked our hunting lodges at the ranch where she goes to paint wildlife, and I've left messages with my caretaker at the island where she paints birds. Nobody's seen her. Sooner or later she'll turn up. She always does. You'll just have to be patient."

"Not my forte."

"Quinn, she's okay. When she's in between museum jobs, she runs around like this. She's always been a free spirit."

"Right." Quinn almost growled. He disliked that the other man could see he was vulnerable and crazed by Kira's disappearance. The need to find her, to find out why she'd vanished, had been building inside him. He couldn't go on if he didn't solve this mystery—and not just because the wedding date loomed.

His one night with Kira had been the closest thing to perfection he'd known since before his dad had died. Never had he experienced with any other woman anything like what he'd shared with Kira. Hell, he hadn't known such closeness was possible. He'd lost himself completely in her, talked to her as he'd never talked to another person.

Even though she'd seemed distant the next morning, he'd thought she'd felt the same wealth of emotion he had and was running scared. But no—something else had made her vanish without a word, even before he'd told her she'd have to marry him if Jaycee didn't. Thinking back, all he could imagine was that she'd felt vulnerable and afraid after their shared night—or that she *had* overheard him talking to Habib.

Then the day after he'd dropped her at her car, Quinn had texted her, as he'd promised, to let her know he'd actually broken it off with Jacinda. She'd never called him back. Nor had she answered her phone since then. She'd never returned to her tiny apartment or her place of employment.

Kira had called her friend Betty to check in, and promised she'd call weekly to keep in touch, but she hadn't given an explanation for her departure or an estimation for when she'd return.

Quinn had to rethink his situation. He'd stopped romancing Jacinda, but he hadn't canceled the wedding because he planned to marry Kira instead. Come Saturday, a thousand people expected him to marry a Murray daughter.

Apparently, his future father-in-law's mind was running along the same worrisome track.

"Quinn, you've got to be reasonable. We've got to call off the wedding," Earl said.

"I'm going to marry Kira."

"You're talking nonsense. Kira's gone. Without a bride, you're going to piss off the very people we want to reassure. Stockholders, clients and employees of Murray Oil. Not to mention—this whole thing is stressing the hell out of Vera, and in her condition that isn't good."

Several months earlier, when Quinn had stalked into Earl's office with enough shares to demand control of Murray Oil, Earl, his eyes blurry and his shoulders slumped, had sat behind his desk already looking defeated.

The older man had wearily confided that his wife was seriously ill. Not only had Earl not cared that Quinn would soon be in charge of Murray Oil, he'd said the takeover was the answer to a prayer. It was time he retired. With Murray Oil in good hands, he could devote himself to his beloved wife, who was sick and maybe dying.

"She's everything to me," he'd whispered. "The way your father was to you and the way your mother was to him before she left him."

"Why tell me—your enemy?" Quinn had asked.

"I don't think of you as my enemy. I never was one to see the world in black or white, the way Kade, your dad, did—the way you've chosen to see it since his death. Whether you believe me or not, I loved your father, and I was sorry about our misunderstanding. You're just like him, you know, so now that I've got my own challenge to face, there's nobody I'd rather turn the company over to than you.

"Vera doesn't want me talking about her illness to friends and family. She can't stand the thought of people, even her daughters, thinking of her as weak and sick. I'm glad I finally have someone I can tell."

Quinn had been stunned. For years, he had hated Earl, had wanted revenge, had looked forward to bringing the man to his knees. But ever since that conversation his feelings had begun to change. The connection he'd found with Kira had hastened that process.

He'd begun to rethink his choices, reconsider his past. Not all his memories of Earl were negative. He could remember some wonderful times hunting and fishing with the blunt-spoken Earl and his dad. As a kid, he'd loved the stories Earl had told around the campfire.

Maybe the bastard had been partially responsible for his father's death. But maybe an equal share of the blame lay with his own father.

Not that Quinn trusted his new attitude. He'd gone too far toward his goal of vengeance not to seize Murray Oil. And he still believed taking a Murray bride would make the acquisition run more smoothly.

"I will get married on Saturday," Quinn said. "All we have to do is convince Kira to come back and marry me."

"Right. But how? We don't even know where she is."

"We don't have to know. All we have to do is motivate her to return," Quinn said softly.

Seabirds raced along the beach, pecking at seaweed. Her jeans rolled to her knees, Kira stood in the shallow surf of Murray Island and wiggled her toes in the cool, damp sand as the wind whipped her hair against her cheeks. Blowing sand stung her bare arms and calves.

Kira needed to make her weekly phone call to Betty after her morning walk—a phone call she dreaded. Each week, it put her back in touch with reality, which was what she wanted to escape from.

Still, she'd known she couldn't stay on the island forever. She'd just thought that solitude would have cleared her head of Quinn by now. But it hadn't. She missed him.

Three weeks of being here alone had changed nothing. None of her confusion or despair about her emotional entanglement with Quinn had lifted.

Maybe if she hadn't been calling Betty to check in, she would be calmer. Betty had told her about Quinn's relentless visits to the restaurant. Thinking about Quinn looking for her had stirred up her emotions and had blocked her artistically. All she could paint was his handsome face.

Well, at least she was painting. When she'd been frustrated while working at the museum, she hadn't even been able to hold a paintbrush.

Since it was past time to call Betty again, she headed for the family beach house. When she climbed the wooden stairs and entered, the wind caught the screen door and banged it behind her.

She turned on her cell phone and climbed to the second floor where the signal and the views of the high surf were better.

Betty answered on the first ring. "You still okay all alone out there?"

"I'm fine. How's Rudy?"

She'd packed her cat and his toys and had taken him to Betty's, much to his dismay.

"Rudy's taken over as usual. Sleeps in my bed. He's right here. He can hear your voice on speakerphone. He's very excited, twitchin' his tail and all." She paused, then, "I worry about you out there alone, Kira."

"Jim's around. He checks on me."

Jim was the island's caretaker. She'd taken him into her confidence and asked him not to tell anyone, not even her father, where she was.

"Well, there's something I need to tell you, something I've been dreadin' tellin' you," Betty began.

"What?"

"That fella of yours, Quinn…"

"He's not my fella."

"Well, he sure acts like he's your guy when he drops by. He's been drillin' the staff, makin' sure you weren't datin' anyone. Said he didn't want to lay claim to a woman who belonged to another."

Lay claim? Kira caught her breath. Just thinking about Quinn in the restaurant looking for her made her breasts swell and her heart throb.

Darn it—would she never forget him?

"Well, today he comes over just as I'm unlocking the door and launches into a tirade about how he's gonna have to break his promise to you and marry your sister, Jaycee! This Saturday!

"I thought it right funny at first, him sayin' that, when he comes by lookin' haunted, askin' after you all the time, so I said up front I didn't buy it. Called him a liar, I did.

"He said maybe he preferred you, but you'd forced his hand. He had to marry a Murray daughter for business reasons, so he would. Everything is set. He told me to read the newspapers, if I didn't believe him. And I did. They're really getting married. It's all over the internet, too."

"What?"

"Tomorrow! Saturday! I know he told you he broke off his wedding plans, but if he did, they're on again. He's every bit as bad as you said. You were right to go away. If I was you, I'd never come back."

So, since he'd never cared which Murray sister he married, he was going to marry Jaycee after all.

Well, she'd stop him. She'd go back—at once—and she'd stop him cold.

Five

A sign in front of the church displayed a calendar that said Murray-Sullivan Wedding: 7:30 p.m.

It was five-thirty as Kira swung into the mostly empty parking lot.

Good. No guests had arrived. She'd made it in time.

The sun was low; the shadows long; the light a rosy gold. Not that she took the time to notice the clarity of the light or the rich green of the grass or the tiny spring leaves budding on the trees. Her heart was pounding. She was perspiring as she hit the brakes and jumped out of her Toyota.

The drive from the coast hadn't taken much more than three hours, but the trip had tired her. Feeling betrayed and yet desperate to find her sister and stop this travesty before it was too late, Kira ran toward the back of the church where the dressing rooms were. Inside, dashing from room to room, she threw open doors, calling her sister's name. Then, suddenly, in the last room, she found Jaycee, wear-

ing a blue cotton dress with a strand of pearls at her throat.
With her blond hair cascading down her back, Jaycee sat
quietly in front of a long, gilt mirror, applying lipstick. She
looked as if she'd been carefully posed by a photographer.

"Jaycee!" Kira cried breathlessly. "At last… Why aren't
you wearing…a wedding dress?"

Then she saw the most beautiful silk gown seeded with
tiny pearls lying across a sofa and a pair of white satin
shoes on the floor.

"Oh, but that's why you're here…to dress… Of course.
Where's Mother? Why isn't Mother here to help you?"

"She's not feeling well. I think she's resting. Mother and
Quinn told me to wait here."

Odd. Usually when it came to organizing any social
affair, their mother had endless reserves of energy that
lasted her until the very end of the event.

"Where are your bridesmaids?"

Turning like an actress compelled by her cue, Jaycee
pressed her lips together and then put her lipstick inside her
blue purse. "I was so worried you wouldn't come," she said.
"I was truly afraid you wouldn't show. We all were. Quinn
most especially. But me, too. He'll be so happy you're here.
I don't know what he would have done if you hadn't gotten
here in time. You don't know how important you are to
him."

Right. That's why he's marrying you without a qualm.

As always, Jaycee worried about everyone she loved.
Kira very much doubted that Quinn would be happy with
her once she finished talking to Jaycee.

Guilt flooded Kira. How would she ever find the words
to explain to her trusting sister why she couldn't marry
Quinn? Jaycee, who'd always been loved by everybody,
probably couldn't imagine there was a soul in the world

who wouldn't love her if she tried hard enough to win him. After all, Daddy had given his blessing.

"You can't marry Quinn today," Kira stated flatly.

"I know that. He told me all about you two. When Daddy asked me to marry Quinn, I tried to tell myself it was the right thing to do. For the family and all. But…when I found out he wanted to marry you…it was such a relief."

"Why did you show up here today if you knew all this?"

"Quinn will…explain everything." Jaycee's eyes widened as the door opened. Kira whirled to tell their visitor that this was a private conversation, but her words died in a convulsive little growl. Quinn, dressed in a tux that set off his broad shoulders and stunning dark looks to heart-stopping perfection, strode masterfully into the room.

Feeling cornered, Kira sank closer to Jaycee. When he saw her, he stopped, his eyes flashing with hurt and anger before he caught her mood and stiffened.

"I was hoping you'd make it in time for the wedding," he said, his deep baritone cutting her to the quick.

"Damn you!" Her throat tightened as she arose. "Liar! How could you do this?"

"I'm thrilled to see you, too, darlin'," he murmured, his gaze devouring her. "You do look lovely."

Kira, who'd driven straight from the island without making a single stop, was wearing a pair of worn, tight jeans and a T-shirt that hugged her curves. She hadn't bothered with makeup or a comb for her tangled hair. She could do nothing but take in a mortified breath at his comment while she stared at his dark face, the face she'd painted so many times even when images of him had blurred through her tears.

"What is the meaning of this?" she screamed.

"There's no need for hysterics, darlin'," he said calmly.

"Don't *darlin'* me! You have no right to call me that!"

she shrieked. "I haven't even begun to show you hysterics! I'm going to tear you limb from limb. Pound you into this tile floor... Skin you alive—"

"Kira, Quinn's been so worried about you. Frantic that you wouldn't show up in time," Jaycee began. "Talk about wedding jitters. He's had a full-blown case..."

"I'll just bet he has!"

"I see we misunderstand each other, Kira. I was afraid of this. Jacinda," he said in a silky tone that maddened Kira further because it made her feel jealous of her innocent sister, "could you give us a minute? I need to talk to Kira alone."

With a quick, nervous glance in Kira's direction, Jaycee said, "Kira, are you sure you'll be okay? You don't look so good."

Kira nodded mutely, wanting to spare Jaycee any necessary embarrassment. So Jaycee slipped out of the room and closed the door quietly.

Her hand raised, Kira bounded toward him like a charging lioness ready to claw her prey, but he caught her wrist and used it to lever her closer.

"Let me go!" she cried.

"Not while you're in such a violent mood, darlin'. You'd only scratch me or do something worse that you'd regret."

"I don't think so."

"This storm will pass, as all storms do. You'll see. Because it's due to a misunderstanding."

"A misunderstanding? I don't think so! You promised you'd break up with my sister, and I, being a fool, believed you. Then you slept with me. How could you go back on a promise like that after what we—"

"I wouldn't. I didn't." His voice was calm, dangerously soft. "I've kept my promise."

"Liar. If I hadn't shown up, you would have married my sister."

"The hell I would have! It was a bluff. How else could I get you to come back to San Antonio? I was going mad not knowing where you were or if you were all right. If you hadn't shown up, I would have looked like a fool, but I wouldn't have married your sister."

"But the newspapers all say you're going to marry her. Here. Today."

"I know what they say because my people wrote the press releases. That was all part of the bluff—to get you here. We'll have to write a correction now, won't we? The only Murray sister I plan to marry today is you, darlin'. If it'll help to convince you, I'll repeat myself on bended knee."

When he began to kneel, she shrieked at him, "Don't you dare...or I'll kick you. This is not a proposal. This is a farce."

"I'm asking you to marry me, darlin'."

He didn't love her. He never would. His was a damaged soul. He'd told her that in plain, hurtful terms right after he'd made love to her.

The details of the conversation she'd overheard came back to her.

"Let me get this straight," she said. "You always intended to marry a Murray daughter."

"And your father suggested Jaycee because he thought she would agree more easily."

"Then I came to your office and asked you not to marry her, and after dinner and sex, you decided one sister was as good as the other. So, why not marry the *easy* sister? Is that about it?"

"Easy?" He snorted. "I wish to hell you were easy, but no, you disappeared for weeks."

"Back to the basics. Marrying one of the Murray daughters is about business and nothing more to you?"

"In the beginning…maybe that was true…"

"I repeat—I heard you talking to Habib, whoever the hell he is, the morning after we made love. And your conversation made it seem that your relationship with me, with any Murray daughter, was still about business. Your voice was cold, matter-of-fact and all too believable."

"Habib works for me. Why would I tell him how I felt when I'd only known you a day and was still reeling, trying to figure it out for myself?"

"Oh, so now you're Mr. Sensitive. Well, I don't believe you, and I won't marry you. I've always dreamed of marrying for love. I know that is an emotion you despise and are incapable of feeling. Maybe that's why you can be so high-handed about forcing me to take my sister's place and marry you. I think you…are despicable…and cold. This whole situation is too cynical for words."

"It's true that our marriage will make Murray Oil employees see this change of leadership in a less hostile way, as for the rest—"

"So, for you, it's business. I will not be bought and sold like so many shares of stock. I am a human being. An educated, Western woman with a woman's dreams and feelings."

"I know that. It's what makes you so enchanting."

"Bull. You've chosen to ride roughshod over me and my family. You don't care what any of us want or feel."

"I do care what you feel. I care too damn much. It's driven me mad these last few weeks, worrying about you. I wished you'd never walked into my office, never made me feel… Hell! You've made me crazy, woman."

Before she had any idea of what he was about to do, he

took a long step toward her. Seizing her, he crushed her against his tall, hard body.

His hands gripping her close, his mouth slanted across hers with enough force to leave her breathless and have her moaning…and then, dear God, as his masterful kiss went on and on and on, she wanted nothing except more of him. Melting, she opened her mouth and her heart. How could she need him so much? She'd missed him terribly—every day they'd been apart.

Needle-sharp thrills raced down her spine. His tongue plunged inside her lips, and soon she was so drunk on his taste and passion, her nails dug into his back. She wanted to be somewhere else, somewhere more private.

She'd missed him. She'd wanted this. She hadn't been able to admit it. His clean, male scent intoxicated her. The length of his all-too-familiar body pressing against hers felt necessary. Every second, asleep and awake, she had thought of him, craved him—craved this. Being held by him only made the need more bittersweet. How could she want such a cold man so desperately?

"We can't feel this, do this," she whispered in a tortured breath even as she clung to him.

"Says who?"

"We're in a church."

His arms tightened their hold. "Marry me, and we can do all we want to each other—tonight…and forever," he said huskily. "It will become a sacred marital right."

How could he say that when he didn't care which Murray sister walked down the aisle as long as it saved him a few million dollars?

The thought hissed through her like cold water splashed onto a fire.

Her parents' love had carried them through many difficulties. Her dad was a workaholic. Her mother was a perfectionist, a status-seeking socialite. But they had always been madly in love.

Kira had grown up believing in the sanctity of marriage. How could she even consider a marriage that would be nothing more than a business deal to her husband?

A potential husband who had lapped up women the way she might attack a box of chocolates. Maybe he temporarily lusted after her, but he didn't love her and never could, as he'd told her. No doubt some other woman would soon catch his fancy.

Even wanting him as she did, she wasn't ready to settle for a marriage based on poor judgment, a momentary sexual connection, shallow lust, revenge and business.

She sucked in a breath and pushed against his massive chest. His grip eased slightly, maybe because the handsome rat thought he'd bent her to his will with his heated words and kisses.

"Listen to me," she said softly. "Are *you* listening?"

"Yes, darlin'."

"I won't marry you. Or any man who could dream up such a cold, cynical scheme."

"How can you call this cold when we're both burning up with desire?" He traced a fingertip along her cheek that made her jump and shiver before she jerked her head away.

"Cheap tricks like that won't induce me to change my mind. There's nothing you can say or do that will convince me. No masterful seduction technique that you honed in other women's bedrooms will do the job, either."

"I wish I had the time to woo you properly and make you believe how special you are."

Special. Now, *there* was a word that hit a nerve. She'd always wanted to feel beloved to those she cared about. How did he know that? It infuriated her that he could guess her sensibilities and so easily use them to manipulate her.

"What you want is revenge and money. If you had all of eternity, it wouldn't be long enough. I won't have you or your loveless deal. That's final."

"We'll see."

His silky baritone was so blatantly confident it sent an icy chill shivering down her spine.

Six

"You told him—the enemy—that Mother might be dying, and you didn't tell me or Jaycee! And you did this behind my back—weeks and weeks ago!"

Kira fisted and unfisted her hands as she sat beside her father in the preacher's library. Rage and hurt shot through her.

"How could you be so disloyal? I've never felt so completely betrayed. Sometimes I feel like a stray you picked up on the side of the road. You didn't really want me—only you have to keep me because it's the right thing to do."

"Nonsense! You're our daughter."

He blanched at her harsh condemnation, and she hung her head in guilt. "I'm sorry," she muttered.

She wanted to weep and scream, but she wouldn't be able to think if she lost all control.

"You know your mother and how she always wants to protect you. I thought only of her when I confided in him."

"First, you sell Jaycee to him because, as always, she's your first choice."

"Kira…"

"Now, it's me."

"Don't blame me. He wants *you!*"

"As if that makes you blameless. Why didn't either of my parents think about protecting their daughters from Quinn?"

"It's complicated. Even if your mother weren't sick, we need someone younger at the top, someone with a clearer vision of the future. Quinn's not what you think. Not what the press thinks. I knew him as a boy. This can be a win-win situation for you both."

"He grew into a vengeful man who hates us."

"You're wrong. He doesn't hate you. You'll never make me believe that. You should have seen how he acted when you disappeared. I think he'll make you a good husband."

"You don't care about that. You don't care about me. You only care about Murray Oil's bottom line, about retiring and being with Mother."

"How can you say that? I care about you, and I care about this family as much as you do. Yes, I need to take care of your mother now, but like I said—I know Quinn. I've watched him. He's good, smart, solid. And he's a brilliant businessman who will be the best possible CEO for Murray Oil during these tumultuous economic times. He's done great things already. If I had time, I'd fill you in on how he helped organize a deal with the EU while you were gone. He's still in the middle of it at the moment."

"For years he's worked to destroy you."

"Hell, maybe he believed that's what he was doing, maybe others bought it, too, but I never did. I don't think *he* knew what was driving him. This company is his heritage, too. And I saw how he was when you were gone.

The man was beside himself. He was afraid you were in trouble. I don't know what happened between the two of you before you ran away, but I know caring when I see it. Quinn cares for you. He's just like his father. You should have seen how Kade loved his wife, Esther. Then you'd know the love Quinn is capable of."

"You think Quinn will come to love me? Are you crazy? Quinn doesn't believe he can love again. The man has lived his life fueled by hate. Hatred for all of us. How many times do I have to repeat it?"

"Maybe so, but the only reason his hatred was so strong was that the love that drove it was just as strong. You're equally passionate. You just haven't found your calling yet." Her father took her hands in his as he continued, "You should have seen him the day he came to tell me he had me by the balls and was set to take over Murray Oil. He could have broken me that day. Instead, he choked when I told him about Vera because he's more decent than he knows. He's ten times the man that his father ever was, that's for sure. Maybe you two didn't meet under ideal circumstances, but he'll make you a good husband."

"You believe that only because you want to believe it. You're as cold and calculating as he is."

"I want what's best for all of us."

"This is a deal to you—just like it is to him. Neither of you care which daughter marries Quinn today, as long as the deal is completed for Murray Oil."

"I suggested Jaycee primarily to avoid a scene like the one we're having, but Quinn wants you. He won't even consider Jaycee now, even though he was willing to marry her before you meddled."

"Oh, so this fiasco is my fault."

"Someday you'll thank me."

"I'm not marrying him. I won't be sacrificed."

"Before you make your decision, your mother wants to talk to you." He pressed a couple of buttons on his phone, and the door behind him opened as if by magic. Her mother's perfectly coiffed blonde head caught the light of the overhead lamp. She was gripping her cell phone with clawlike hands.

She looked so tiny. Why hadn't Kira noticed how thin and colorless her once-vital mother had become? How frail and tired she looked?

"Dear God," Kira whispered as she got up and folded her precious mother into her arms. She felt her mother's ribs and spine as she pressed her body closer. Her mother was fading away right before her eyes.

"Please," her mother whispered. "I'm not asking you to do this for me, but for your father. I need all my strength to fight this illness. He can't be worried about Murray Oil. Or you. Or Jaycee. I've always been the strong one, you know. I can't fight this if I have to worry about him. And I can't leave him alone. He'd be lost without me."

"I—I..."

"I'm sure your father's told you there's a very important international deal with the EU on the table right now. It can make or break our company."

"*His* company."

"Your father and I and the employees of Murray Oil need your help, Kira. Your marriage to Quinn would endorse his leadership both here and abroad. Have I ever asked you for anything before?"

Of course she had. She'd been an ambitious and very demanding mother. Kira had always hoped that when she married and had children, she'd finally be part of a family where she felt as if she belonged, where she was accepted, flaws and all. How ironic that when her parents finally needed her to play a role they saw as vital to their survival, their need trampled on her heartfelt dream to be at the core of her own happy family.

Would she ever matter to her husband the way her mother mattered to her father? Not if the man who was forcing her to marry him valued her only as a business prize. Once Quinn had Murray Oil under his control, how long would she be of any importance to him?

Still, what choice did she have? For the first time ever, her family really needed her. And she'd always wanted that above all things.

"I don't want to marry you! But yes!" she spat at Quinn after he had ushered her into one of the private dressing rooms. She'd spun around to face him in the deadly quiet. "*Yes!* I will marry you, since you insist on having your answer today."

"Since I insist we marry today!"

Never had she seemed lovelier than with her dark, heavily lashed eyes glittering with anger and her slender hands fisted defiantly on her hips. He was so glad to have found her. So glad she was all right. So glad she'd agreed without wasting any more precious time. Once she was his, they'd get past this.

"Then I'll probably hate you forever for forcing me to make such a terrible bargain."

Her words stabbed him with pain, but he steeled himself not to show it. She looked mad enough to spit fire and stood at least ten feet from him so he couldn't touch her.

Looking down, staring anywhere but at her, he fought to hide the hurt and relief he felt at her answer, as well as the regret he felt for having bullied her.

Bottom line—she would be his. Today. The thought of any man touching her as Quinn had touched her their one night together seemed a sacrilege worthy of vengeful murder.

"Good. I'm glad that's finally settled and we can move on," he said in a cool tone that masked his own seething passions. "I've hired people to help you get ready. Beauticians. Designers. I selected a wedding gown that I hope you'll like, and I have a fitter here in case I misjudged your size."

"You did all that?" Her narrow brows arched with icy contempt. "You were that sure I'd say yes? You thought I was some doll you could dress up in white satin..."

"Silk, actually, and no, I don't think you're some doll—" He stopped. He wasn't about to admit how desperate he'd felt during the dark days of her absence, or how out of control, even though his silence only seemed to make her angrier.

"Look, just because you bullied me into saying yes doesn't mean I like the way you manipulated my family into taking your side. And, since this is strictly a business deal to all of you, I want you to know it's nothing but a business deal to me, too. So, I'm here by agreeing to a marriage in name only. The only reasons I'm marrying you are to help my father and mother and Murray Oil and to save Jaycee from you."

His lips thinned. "There's too much heat in you. You won't be satisfied with that kind of marriage...any more than I will."

"Well, I won't marry you unless you agree to it."

He would have agreed to sell his soul to the devil to have her. "Fine," he said. "Suit yourself, but when you change your mind, I won't hold you to your promise."

"I won't change my mind."

He didn't argue the point or try to seduce her. He'd

make the necessary concessions to get her to the altar. He'd pushed her way too far already.

He was willing to wait, to give her the time she needed. He didn't expect it would be long before he'd have her in his bed once more. And perhaps it was for the best that they take a break from the unexpected passion they'd found.

Maybe he wanted her to believe his motive for marrying her was business related, but it was far from the truth. Need—pure, raw, unadulterated need—was what drove him. If they didn't make love for a while, perhaps he could get control over all his emotions.

After they'd made love the last time, he'd felt too much, had felt too bound to her. Her power over him scared the hell out of him. She'd left him just as carelessly as his own mother had left his father, hadn't she?

He needed her like the air he breathed. Kira had simply become essential.

But he wasn't about to tell her that. No way could he trust this overwhelming need for any woman. Hadn't his father's love for Quinn's own mother played the largest part in his father's downfall? And then his own love for his father had crushed him when his father died.

Grief was too big a price to pay for love. He never wanted to be weak and needy like that again.

Seven

"You look...absolutely amazing," her mother said, sounding almost as pleased as she usually did when she complimented Jaycee. "Don't frown! You know you do!"

In a trancelike daze, Kira stared at the vision in the gilt mirror. How had Quinn's beauty experts made her look like herself and yet so much better? They'd tugged and pulled, clipped and sprayed unmercifully, and now here she was, a sexy, glowing beauty in a diaphanous silk gown that clung much too revealingly. The dress flattered her slim figure perfectly. How had he known her exact size and what would most become her?

All those blondes, she told herself. He understood glamour and women, not her. The dress wasn't about her. He wanted her to be like them.

Still, until this moment, she'd never realized how thoroughly into the Cinderella fantasy she'd been. Not that she would ever admit that, on some deep level, he'd pleased her.

"How can I walk down the aisle in a dress you can see straight through?"

"You're stunning. The man has flawless taste."

"Another reason to hate him," Kira mumbled, brushing aside her mother's hard-won approval and pleasure for fear of having it soften her attitude toward Quinn.

"Haven't I always told you, you should have been playing up your assets all along," her mother said.

"Straight guys aren't supposed to know how to do stuff like this."

"Count yourself lucky your man has such a rare talent. You'll have to start letting him dress you. Maybe he knows how to bring out your best self in other areas, as well. If he does, you'll amaze yourself."

The way he had during their one night together. A shiver traced through her. "May I remind you that this is not a real marriage?"

"If you'd quit saying that in such a sulky, stubborn tone, maybe it would become one, and very soon. He's very handsome. I'll bet there isn't a single woman in this church who wouldn't trade places with you."

"He doesn't love me."

"Well, why don't you start talking to him in a sweet voice? More like the one that you always use with that impossible cat of yours?"

"Maybe because he's not my loyal, beloved pet. Maybe because being bullied into a relationship with him does not make me feel sweet and tender."

"Well, if you ask me, the men you've chosen freely weren't much to brag about. Quinn is so well educated and well respected."

A few minutes later, when the wedding march started, Kira glided down the aisle in white satin slippers holding on to her father's arm. When she heard awed gasps from the guests, she lifted her eyes from the carpet, but in the sea of faces it was Quinn's proud smile alone that made her heart leap and brought a quick, happy blush to her cheeks.

Then her tummy flipped as their souls connected in that uncanny way that made her feel stripped bare. Fortunately, her father angled himself between them, and she got a brief reprieve from Quinn's mesmerizing spell.

Not that it was long before her father had handed her over to her bridegroom where she became her awkward, uncertain self again. As she stood beside Quinn at the altar, she fidgeted while they exchanged rings and vows. With a smile, he clasped her hand in his. Threading her fingers through his, he held them still. Somehow, his warm touch reassured her, and she was able to pledge herself to him forever in a strong, clear voice.

This isn't a real marriage, she reminded herself, even as that bitter truth tore at her heart.

But the tall man beside her, the music, the church and the incredibly beautiful dress, combined with the memory of her own radiance in the mirror, made her doubt what she knew to be true. Was she a simple-minded romantic after all, or just a normal girl who wanted to marry a man she loved?

After the preacher told Quinn he could kiss his bride, Quinn's arms encased her slim body with infinite gentleness. His eyes went dark in that final moment before he lowered his beautifully sculpted mouth to hers. Despite her intention not to react to his lips, to feel nothing when he kissed her, her blood pulsed. Gripping his arms, she leaned into him.

"We'd better make this count because if you have your way, it will probably be a while before I convince you to let me kiss you again," he teased huskily.

She threw her arms around his warm, bronzed neck, her

fingers stroking his thick hair, and drew his head down. Fool that she was, it felt glorious to be in his arms as he claimed her before a thousand witnesses.

Such a ceremonial kiss shouldn't mean anything, she told herself. He was just going through the motions. As was she.

"Darlin'," he murmured. "Sweet darlin' Kira. You are incredibly beautiful, incredibly dear. I want you so much. No bridegroom has ever felt prouder of his bride."

The compliment brought her startled eyes up to his, and his tender expression fulfilled her long-felt secret desire to be special to someone. For one shining instant, she believed the dream. If a man as sophisticated as he was could really be proud of her and want her...

He didn't, of course... Oh, but if only he could...

Then his mouth was on hers. His tongue inside the moist recesses of her lips had her blood heating and her breath shuddering in her lungs. Her limbs went as limp as a rag doll's. When she felt his heart hammering against her shoulder blade, she let him pull her even closer.

The last thing she wanted was to feel this swift rush of warm pleasure, but she couldn't stop herself. How could a single, staged kiss affect her so powerfully?

He was the first to pull away. His smile was slow and sweet. "Don't forget—the last thing I want is for our marriage to be business-only," he whispered against her ravaged lips. "You can change your mind anytime, darlin'. Anytime. Nothing would please me more than to take you to my bed again."

"Well, I won't change my mind! Not ever!" she snapped much too vehemently.

He laughed and hugged her close. "You will. I should warn you that nothing appeals to me more than a challenge."

After a lengthy photography session—she was surprised that he wanted photos of a wedding that couldn't possibly mean anything to him—they were driven by limousine to the reception, held at his opulent club in an older section of San Antonio.

Once again he'd planned everything—decorations in the lavish ballroom, the menu, the band—with enough attention to detail that her critical mother was thoroughly impressed and radiantly aglow with pride. Vera sailed through the glittering throng like a bejeweled queen among awed subjects as she admired the banks of flowers, frozen sculptures and the sumptuous food and arrangements. Kira was secretly pleased Quinn had at least married her under circumstances that gave her mother, who loved to impress, so much pleasure.

With a few exceptions, the majority of the guests were employees and clients of Murray Oil. The few personal friends and family attending included Quinn's uncle Jerry, who'd been his best man, and her friend Betty. The guest list also included a few important people from the Texas art world, mostly museum directors, including Gary Whitehall, the former boss who'd let her go...for daring to have an opinion of her own.

Since the wedding was a business affair, Kira was surprised that Quinn had allowed his employees to bring their children, but he had. And no one was enjoying themselves more than the kids. They danced wildly and chased each other around the edges of the dance floor, and when a father spoke harshly to the little flower girl for doing cartwheels in her long velvet gown, Quinn soothed the child.

Watching the way the little girl brightened under his tender ministrations, Kira's heart softened.

"He's very good with children," Betty whispered into her ear. "He'll make a wonderful father."

"This is not a real marriage."

"You could have fooled me. I get all mushy inside every time he looks at you. He's *so* good-looking."

"He's taken over my life."

"Well, I'd be glad to take him off your hands. I think he's hunky. And so polite. Did I tell you how nice he was to Rudy after he found out the reason the beast wouldn't stop meowing was because he missed you? He sat down with that cat and commiserated. Made me give the beast some tuna."

"I'll bet he got you to feed him, too."

"Well, every time Quinn came to the restaurant he did sit down with me and whoever was waiting tables, like he was one of us. He bragged on my pies."

"Which got him free pies I bet."

"His favorite is the same as yours."

"Your gooey lemon meringue?"

"I thought he was sweet to remember to invite me to the wedding. He called this evening after you showed up."

Betty hushed when Quinn appeared at his bride's side and stayed, playing the attentive groom long after his duties in the receiving line ended. Even when several beauties— one a flashy blonde he'd once dated named Cristina, whom he'd apparently hired as a junior executive—came up and flirted boldly, he'd threaded his fingers through Kira's and tucked her closer.

For more than an hour, ignoring all others, he danced only with Kira. He was such a strong partner, she found herself enjoying the reception immensely as he whirled her around the room. She could see the admiring glances following them. He smiled down at her often, no doubt to give the appearance that she delighted him. The women who'd flirted with him watched him with intense interest, especially Cristina, whose lovely mouth began to pout.

"I've never been much of a dancer," Kira confessed during a slow number.

"You could've fooled me. Just goes to show that all you need is a little self-confidence."

Had his attentiveness given her that, at least briefly? When Gary Whitehall's gaze met hers over Quinn's broad shoulder, he smiled tightly. As Quinn's wife, she'd taken a huge step up in the art world. Was Gary wishing he'd let someone else go other than her when the budget had been tight? Why had Quinn included him on the guest list?

After a fast number, when Kira admitted she was thirsty, Quinn left her to get champagne. Seeing his chance, Gary rushed up to her.

"You look lovely," he said, smiling in the way he used to smile at major artists and important donors. How rare had been the smiles and compliments he'd bestowed on his lowly curator for her hard work. "I'm very happy for you," he said.

She nodded, embarrassed to be so pleased that her marriage had won his respect.

"If I can do anything for you, anything at all, just call me. I am rewriting your letter of recommendation. Not that you'll need to work now."

"I intend to work again. I loved my job."

"Your husband has been most generous to the museum. We value his friendship and expertise almost as much as we will value yours—as his wife," he gushed. "I have a feeling we may have a position for a curator opening up soon. If so, I'll give you a call."

She thought about what Gary had said about a position possibly being available and was surprised she was so pleased. Maybe…she would consider working for him again…if he made her the right offer. She would, however, demand to have more power.

Stunned, she stared at him. Then Quinn returned with her champagne. The two men shook hands and exchanged pleasantries. When Quinn made it clear he preferred his bride's conversation to art talk, Gary quickly eased himself back into the crowd. But every time after that conversation, when their eyes met, Gary smiled at her.

For a man who supposedly hated her family, Quinn was excessively attentive to her mother and father and Jaycee. He talked to them, ordered them wine and appetizers, acted as if he actually wished to please them. He was especially solicitous of her mother, who positively glowed.

Kira watched him during dinner, and his warm smiles and polite comments rang with sincerity. If she hadn't known better, she wouldn't have believed he was simply acting a part in order to reassure oil company clients and executives that Murray Oil was in good hands.

Never had a bridegroom appeared more enthusiastic, even when his uncle Jerry congratulated him on his marriage.

"Kira, he's had his nose to the grindstone so long, we were beginning to think that's all he'd ever do," Jerry said. "We'd given up on you, son. Now I see you just hadn't met the right girl. Sooner or later, if we're lucky, love comes our way. The trick is to know it and appreciate it. When you fall in love, wanting to spend the rest of your life with the same woman doesn't seem that hard to imagine."

Quinn stared at her as if he agreed. The two men shook hands again and laughed. But since Quinn's heart wasn't really in their marriage, she wondered how soon he'd give up trying to pretend to people like his uncle. After that, when she felt herself too charmed by one of Quinn's thoughtful smiles or gestures, she reminded herself that she'd be a fool if she fell for his act. Their marriage was a business deal. She didn't matter to him. She never would.

All too soon the dinner and dancing came to an end, and she and Quinn had changed into street clothes and were dashing out to his limo while cheering guests showered them with birdseed. When someone threw seeds straight at her eyes, and a tear streamed down her cheek, Quinn took out his monogrammed handkerchief and dabbed her face while everybody cheered.

She expected to be driven to his loft. Instead, the limo whisked them to his sleek private jet, which had been prepared for flight and was waiting outside a hangar at the San Antonio International Airport.

"Where are we going?" she asked as he helped her out into the blinding glare of dozens of flashes.

"Honeymoon," he whispered, his mouth so close to her ear she felt the heat of his breath. Her heart raced until she reminded herself he was only staging a romantic shot for the press.

Putting his arm around her, he faced the reporters, who asked him questions about his pending international oil deal as well as his marriage.

With abundant charm and smiles, he answered a few and then, grabbing her by the elbow, propelled her into his jet.

"Surely a honeymoon isn't necessary," she said when they were safely on board.

He smiled down at her. "A man only marries once."

"Like that reporter asked—how can you afford the time when you're working on that important EU deal?"

"You have to make time…for what's important."

"So, why did you notify the press about our honeymoon? Was it only so the EU people would know you married into the Murray family?"

"Why don't you relax? Step one, quit asking so many questions. Step two, just enjoy."

"You're thorough. I'll have to give you that. Even so,

how can I leave town when I haven't even packed for a trip," she said. "Besides, I have a cat—Rudy. I promised Betty I'd relieve her... He's been crying for me."

"I know. Rudy's all taken care of. Jacinda's going to look after him at your apartment. So, he'll be on his own turf. I bought him a case of tuna."

"You shopped for Rudy?"

"Okay—so I sent my assistant. And your mother helped me shop and pack for you."

"I'll bet she loved that."

"She did—although I did make certain key choices."

"Such as?"

"The lingerie and bikinis."

"Lingerie? I'm not much for lingerie! Or bikinis!"

"Good. Then you'll be exquisite in nothing. You slept in my arms like that all night, remember."

Hot color flooded her face. "Don't!"

"With your legs wrapped silkily around me," he added. "You were so warm and sweet, I can't believe you really intend to sleep alone tonight."

The images he aroused in her, coupled with his warm gaze and sexy grin, made her blood hum.

"I meant I feel bad about going away again so soon without telling Betty."

"Already done. Betty's fine with the idea."

"You *are* thorough."

When her temples began to throb, Kira squeezed her eyes shut. "Did everyone, absolutely everyone, know I was getting married to you today before I did?"

"Not me, darlin'. I was scared sick you wouldn't turn up or that you'd order me straight to hell after I proposed."

Had he really felt that way? Did he care a little?

No! She couldn't let herself ask such questions.

Or care at all what the answers might be.

Eight

An hour later, after a flight to the coast and a brief but exciting helicopter ride over Galveston Island, they dropped out of the night sky onto the sleek, upper deck of the white floating palace he kept moored at the Galveston marina. She took his arm when the rotors stopped and sucked in a breath as he helped her onto his yacht. Gusts of thick, humid air that smelled of the sea whipped her clothes and hair.

Promising to give her a tour of the megayacht the next day, the captain led them down a flight of steep, white stairs and through a wood-lined corridor to Quinn's master stateroom. Clearly the captain hadn't been told that they would not be sharing a room. Crewmen followed at a brisk pace to deliver their bags.

Once alone with Quinn in his palatial, brass-studded cabin, her brows knitted in concern as she stared at the mountain of bags.

"Don't worry. If you really insist on sleeping alone, I'll move mine."

Shooting a nervous glance toward his big bed, she felt her body heat.

Above the headboard hung a magnificent painting of a nude blonde by an artist she admired. The subject was lying on her tummy across a tumble of satin sheets, her slender back arched to reveal ample breasts. Long-lashed, come-hither eyes compelled the viewer not to look away. Surely such a wanton creature would never send her husband away on their wedding night.

"Last chance to change your mind," he said.

Feeling strangely shy, Kira crossed her arms over her own breasts and shook her head. "So, where will you sleep?"

"Next door." There was a mesmerizing intensity in his eyes. "Would you like to see my room?"

She twisted her hands. "I'll be just fine right here. So, if that's settled, I guess we'll see each other in the morning."

"Right." He hesitated. "If you need anything, all you have to do is punch this button on your bedside table and one of the staff will answer. If you want me, I'll leave my door unlocked. Or, if you prefer me to come to you, you could ring through on that phone over there."

"Thanks."

He turned, opened the door, shoved his bags into the passageway and stepped outside. When the door slammed behind him, and she was alone with his come-hither blonde, a heavy emotion that felt too much like disappointment gripped her.

To distract herself, she studied the painting for another moment, noting that the artist had used linseed oil most effectively to capture the effect of satin.

Feeling a vague disquiet as she considered the nude,

she decided the best thing to do was shower and get ready for bed. As she rummaged in her suitcase, she found all sorts of beautiful clothes that she never would have picked out. Still, as she touched the soft fabrics and imagined her mother shopping for such things without her there to discourage such absurd purchases, she couldn't help smiling. Her mother had always wanted to dress Kira in beautiful things, but being a tomboy, Kira had preferred jeans and T-shirts.

What was the point of fancy clothes for someone who lived as she had, spending time in art vaults, or painting, or waiting tables? But now, she supposed, for however long she was married to a billionaire with his own jet and megayacht, she would run in different circles and have fundraisers and parties to attend. Maybe she did need to upgrade her wardrobe.

Usually, she slept in an overlarge, faded T-shirt. In her suitcase all she found for pajamas were thin satin gowns and sheer robes, the kind that would cling so seductively she almost regretted she wouldn't be wearing them for Quinn.

Instead of the satin gown, which reminded her too much of the blonde above the bed, she chose black lace. Had he touched the gown, imagining her in it, when he'd picked it out? As the gossamer garment slipped through her fingers she shivered.

Go to bed. Don't dwell on what might have been. He's ruined enough of your day and night as it is.

But how not to think of him as she stripped and stepped into her shower? What was he doing next door? Was his tall, bronzed body naked, too? Her heart hammered much too fast.

Lathering her body underneath a flow of warm water, she imagined him doing the same in his own shower. Leaning against the wet tile wall, she grew hotter and hotter as the water streamed over her. She stood beneath the spray until her fingers grew too numb to hold the slippery bar of soap. When it fell, she snapped out of her spell.

Drying off and then slipping into the black gown, she slid into his big bed with a magazine. Unable to do more than flip pages and stare unseeingly at the pictures because she couldn't stop thinking about Quinn, she eventually drifted to sleep. But once asleep, she didn't dream of him.

Instead, she dreamed she was a small child in her pink bedroom with its wall-to-wall white carpet. All her books were lined up just perfectly, the way her mother liked them to be, in her small white bookcase beneath the window.

Somewhere in the house she heard laughter and hushed endearments, the sort of affection she'd never been able to get enough of. Then her door opened and her parents rushed inside her bedroom. Only they didn't take her into their arms as they usually did. Her mother was cooing over a bundle she held against her heart, and her father was staring down at what her mother held as if it were the most precious thing in the world.

She wanted them to look at her like that.

"Kira, we've brought your new baby sister, Jaycee, for a visit."

A baby sister? "Where did she come from?"

"The hospital."

"Is that where you got me?"

Her mother paled. Her father looked as uneasy as her mother, but he nodded.

What was going on?

"Do you love me, too?" Kira whispered.

"Yes, of course," her father said. "You're our big girl now, so your job will be to help us take care of Jaycee.

She's *our* special baby. We're all going to work hard to take very good care of Jaycee."

Suddenly, the bundle in her mother's arms began to shriek frantically.

"What can I do?" Kira had said, terrified as she ran toward them. "How can I help? Tell me what to do!"

But they'd turned away from her. "Why don't you just play," her father suggested absently.

Feeling lonely and left out as she eyed her dolls and books, she slowly backed away from them and walked out of her room, down the tall stairs to the front door, all the while hoping their concerned voices would call her back as they usually did. She wasn't supposed to be downstairs at night.

But this time, they didn't call her. Instead, her parents carried the new baby into a bedroom down the hall and stayed with her.

They had a new baby. They didn't need her anymore.

Kira opened the big front door. They didn't notice when she stepped outside. Why should they? They had Jaycee, who was special. They didn't care about Kira anymore. Maybe they'd never really cared.

Suddenly, everything grew black and cold, and a fierce wind began to blow, sweeping away everything familiar. The house vanished, and she was all alone in a strange, dark wood with nobody to hear her cries. Terrified, she ran deeper into the woods.

If her family didn't love her anymore, if nobody loved her, she didn't know what she would do.

Hysterical, she began sobbing their names. "Mother! Daddy! Somebody! Please…love me. I want to be special, too…"

Quinn opened her door and hurled himself into her stateroom.

"Kira!" He switched on a light. She blinked against the blinding glare of gold with heavy-lidded eyes.

"Are you okay?" he demanded. "Wake up!"

"Quinn?" Focusing on his broad shoulders, she blinked away the last remnants of that terrifying forest. He was huge and shirtless and so starkly handsome in the half shadows she hissed in a breath.

Her husband. What a fool she'd been to send him away when that was the last thing she really wanted.

When he sat down on the bed, she flung herself against his massive bare chest and clung. He felt so hard and strong and hot.

Snugging her close against his muscular body, he rocked her gently and spoke in soothing tones. "There…there…"

Wrapped in his warmth, she almost felt safe…and loved.

"I was a little girl again. Only I ran away and got lost. In a forest."

He petted her hair as his voice soothed her. "You were only dreaming."

She stared up at his shadowed face. In the aftermath of her dream, she was too open to her need of him. Her grip on him tightened. She felt his breath hitch and his heart thud faster. If only *he* loved her…maybe the importance of her childhood fears would recede.

"Darlin', it was just a dream. You're okay."

Slowly, because he held her, the horror of feeling lost and alone diminished and reality returned.

She was on his megayacht. In Galveston. He'd forced her to marry him and come on a honeymoon. She was in his bed where she'd been sleeping alone. This was supposed to be their wedding night, but she'd sent him away.

Yet somehow *she* was the one who felt lonely and rejected.

She liked being cradled in his strong arms, against his

virile body. Too much. She grew conscious of the danger of letting him linger in her bedroom.

"You want me to go?" he whispered roughly.

No. She wanted to cling to him…to be adored by him.… Another impossible dream.

When she hesitated, he said, "If you don't send me packing, I will take this as an invitation."

"It's no invitation," she finally murmured, but sulkily. Her heart wasn't in her statement.

"How come you don't sound sure?" He ran a rough palm across her cheek. Did she only imagine the intimate plea in his voice? Was he as lonely as she was?

Even as she felt herself softening under his affectionate touch and gentle tone, she forced herself to remember all the reasons she'd be a fool to trust him. Squeezing her eyes shut, she took a deep breath. "Thanks for coming, but go! Please—just go."

She felt his body tighten as he stared into her eyes. Time ticked for an endless moment before he released her.

Without a word he got up and left.

Alone again, she felt she might burst with sheer longing. When she didn't sleep until dawn, she blamed him for not going farther than the room next to hers. He was too close. Knowing that all she had to do was go to him increased her frustration. Because he'd made it clear he would not send her away.

Twisting and turning, she fought to settle into slumber, but could not. First, she was too hot for the covers. Then she was so cold she'd burrowed under them.

It was nearly dawn when she finally did sleep. Then, after less than an hour, loud voices in the passageway startled her into grouchy wakefulness. As she buried her head in her pillow, her first thought was of Quinn. He'd probably slept like a baby.

When the sun climbed high and his crewmen began shouting to one another on deck, she strained to hear Quinn's voice among theirs shouts, but didn't.

Sitting up, alone, she pulled the covers to her throat. Surely he couldn't still be sleeping. Where was he?

A dark thought hit her. Last night he'd left her so easily, when what she'd craved was for him to stay. Had she already served her purpose by marrying him? Was he finished with her?

Feeling the need for a strong cup of coffee, Kira slipped into a pair of tight, white shorts and a skimpy, beige knit top. Outside, the sky was blue, the sun brilliant. Normally, when she wasn't bleary from lack of sleep, Kira loved water, boats and beaches. Had Quinn been in love with her, a honeymoon on his luxurious yacht would have been exceedingly romantic. Instead, she felt strange and alone and much too needily self-conscious.

Was his crew spying on her? Did they know Quinn hadn't slept with her? Did they pity her?

Anxious to find Quinn, Kira grabbed a white sweater and left the stateroom. When he didn't answer her knock, she cracked open his door. A glance at the perfectly made spread and his unopened luggage told her he'd spent the night elsewhere. Pivoting, she stepped back into the corridor so fast she nearly slammed headlong into a crewman.

"May I help you, Mrs. Sullivan?"

"Just taking a private tour," she lied. On the off chance he'd think she knew where she was going, she strode purposefully past him down the wood-lined passageway.

Outside, the gulf stretched in endless sapphire sparkle toward a shimmering horizon. Not that she paid much attention to the dazzling view. Intent on finding Quinn, she was too busy opening every door on the sumptuously appointed decks. Too proud to ask the numerous crew members she passed for help, she averted her eyes when she chanced to meet one of them for fear they'd quiz her.

The yacht seemed even bigger on close inspection. So far she'd found six luxury staterooms, a cinema, multiple decks, a helipad and a grand salon.

Just when she was about to give up her search for Quinn, she opened a door on the uppermost deck and found him slumped over a desk in a cluttered office. Noting the numerous documents scattered on chairs, desks, tables and even the floor, she crossed the room to his side. Unfinished cups of coffee sat atop the jumbled stacks. Obviously, he'd worked through the night on a caffeine high.

At the sight of his exhausted face, her heart constricted. Even as she smoothed her hand lightly through his rumpled hair, she chastised herself for feeling sympathy for him. Hadn't he bullied her into their forced, loveless marriage?

Now that she knew where he was, she should go, order herself coffee and breakfast, read her magazine in some pristine chaise lounge, sunbathe—in short, ignore him. Thinking she would do just that, she stepped away from him. Then, driven by warring emotions she refused to analyze, she quickly scampered back to his side.

Foolishly, she felt tempted to neaten his office, but since she didn't know what went where, she sank into the chair opposite his. Bringing her knees against her chest, she hugged them tightly and was pleased when he slept another hour under her benevolent guardianship. Then, without warning, his beautiful eyes snapped open and seared her.

"What the hell are you doing here?" he demanded.

She nearly jumped out of her chair. "He awakens—like a grumpy old bear," she teased.

Managing a lopsided grin, he ran a hand through his

spiked, rumpled hair. "You were a bit grumpy...the morning after...you slept with me in San Antonio, as I recall."

"Don't remind me of that disastrous night, please."

"It's one of my fondest memories," he said softly.

"I said don't!"

"I love it when you blush like that. It makes you look so...cute. You should have awakened me the minute you came in."

"How could I be so heartlessly cruel when you came to my rescue in the middle of the night? If you couldn't sleep, it was my fault."

When his beautiful white teeth flashed in a teasing grin, she couldn't help smiling back at him.

"I could bring you some coffee. Frankly, I could use a cup myself," she said.

He sat up straighter and stretched. "Sorry this place is such a mess, but as I'm not through here, I don't want anybody straightening it up yet."

She nodded. "I sort of thought that might be the case."

"What about breakfast...on deck, then? I have a crew ready to wait on us hand and foot. They're well trained in all things—food service...emergencies at sea..."

"They didn't come when I screamed last night," she said softly. "You did."

"Only because you didn't call for their help on the proper phone."

"So, it's my fault, is it?" Where had the lilt in her light tone come from?

Remembering how safe she'd felt in his arms last night, a fierce tenderness toward him welled up in her heart. He must have sensed what she felt, because his eyes flared darkly before he looked away.

Again, she wished this were a real honeymoon, wished that he loved her rather than only lusted for her, wished that she was allowed to love him back. If only she hadn't demanded separate bedrooms, then she would be lying in his arms looking forward to making love with him again this morning.

At the thought, her neck grew warm. She'd been wishing for the wrong stuff her whole life. It was time she grew up and figured out what her life was to be about. The sooner she got started on that serious journey, one that could never include him, the better.

Nine

Breakfast on deck with his long-limbed bride in her sexy short shorts was proving to be an unbearable torture. She squirmed when his gaze strayed to her lips or her breasts or when it ran down those long, lovely legs.

If only he could forget how she'd clung to him last night or how her big eyes had adored him when he'd first woken up this morning.

"I wish you wouldn't stare so," she said as she licked chocolate off a fingertip. "It makes me feel self-conscious about eating this and making such a mess."

"Sorry," he muttered.

He tried to look away, but found he could not. What else was there to look at besides endless sapphire dazzle? Why shouldn't he enjoy watching her greedily devour her fresh-baked croissants and *pain du chocolat*? The way she licked chocolate off her fingers made him remember her mouth and tongue on him that night in his loft. *Torture.*

Even though he was sitting in the shade and the gulf breeze was cool, his skin heated. His bride was too sexy for words.

If he were to survive the morning without grabbing her like a besotted teenager and making a fool of himself, he needed to quickly get back to his office and the EU deal.

But he knew he wouldn't be able to concentrate on the deal while his forbidden bride was aboard. No. He'd go to the gym and follow his workout with a long, cold shower. Only then would he attempt another try at the office.

Dear God, why was it that ever since she'd said no sex, bedding her was all he could think about?

With the fortitude that was so much a part of his character, he steeled himself to endure her beauty and her provocative sensuality, at least until breakfast was over and they parted ways.

"So, are we heading somewhere in particular?" she asked playfully.

"Do you like to snorkel?"

"I do, but I've only snorkeled in lakes and shallow coves in the Caribbean."

"Once we get into really deep water, the gulf will be clear. I thought we'd snorkel off one of my oil rigs. It's always struck me as ironic the way marine life flourishes around a rig. You're in for a treat."

Her brief smile charmed him. "I read somewhere that rigs act like artificial reefs." She stopped eating her orange. "But you don't need to interrupt your precious work to entertain me."

"I'll set my own work schedule, if you don't mind."

"You're the boss, my lord and master. Sorry I keep forgetting that all-important fact." Again her playful tone teased him.

"Right." He smiled grimly. What could he say?

They lapsed into an uncomfortable silence. Focusing on his eggs and bacon, he fought to ignore her. Not that he didn't want to talk to her, because he did. Very much. But small talk with his bride was not proving to be an easy matter.

"I'd best get busy," he said when he'd finished his eggs and she her orange.

"Okay. Don't worry about me. Like I said, I can entertain myself. I love the water. As you know, I spent the past few weeks on Murray Island. I don't know where we are, but we probably aren't that far from it."

Scanning the horizon, he frowned. He didn't like remembering how much her stay at her family's isolated island had worried him.

How had he become so attached—or whatever the hell he was—to her so fast? They'd only had one night together!

Biting out a terse goodbye that made her pretty smile falter, he stood abruptly. Pivoting, he headed to his gym and that icy shower while she set off to her stateroom.

The gym and shower didn't do any good. No sooner did he return to his office on the upper deck than who should he find sunbathing right outside his door practically naked but his delectable bride.

She lay on a vivid splash of red terry cloth atop one of his chaise lounges, wearing the white thong bikini he'd picked out for her while under the influence of a lurid male fantasy.

He'd imagined her in it. Hell, yes, he had. But not like this—not with her body forbidden to him by her decree and his unwillingness to become any more attached to her. He would never have bought those three tiny triangles if he'd had any idea what torture watching her would give him.

Clenching his fists, he told himself to snap the blinds shut and forget her. Instead, mesmerized, he crossed his office with the long strides of a large, predatory cat and stood at a porthole, staring at her hungrily, ravenous for whatever scraps of tenderness the sexy witch might bestow. He willed her to look at him.

She flipped a magazine page carelessly and continued to read with the most maddening intensity. Not once did she so much as glance his way.

Damn her.

She was on her tummy in the exact position of the girl in the painting over his bed. He watched her long, dark hair glint with fiery highlights and blow about her slim, bare shoulders. He watched her long, graceful fingers flip more pages and occasionally smooth back flying strands of her hair. Every movement of her slim wrist had her dainty silver bracelet flashing.

Was she really as cool and collected as she appeared?

How could she be, when she'd given herself to him so quickly and completely that first night? Her eyes had shone with desire, and she'd trembled and quivered at his touch. She hadn't faked her response. He'd bet his life on it. He would never have forced her to marry him if he'd thought her cold and indifferent.

And last night he'd definitely felt her holding on to him as if she didn't want to let go.

So, she must be clinging to her position of abstinence out of principle. Wasn't she turning those pages much too fast? Was she even reading that magazine? Or was she as distracted as he was? Did she sense him watching her and take perverse delight in her power over him?

Damn the fates that had sent her to him!

Always, before Kira, he'd gone for voluptuous blondes with modern morals, curvy women who knew how to dress, women who thought their main purpose was to please a man. Women with whom he'd felt safe because they'd wanted his money and position more than they'd valued his heart.

This slim, coltishly long-limbed girl hadn't yet learned what she was about or even how to please herself, much less how to seduce a man. But her innocence in these matters appealed to him.

Why?

Again, he told himself to forget her, but when he went to his desk, he just sat there for a full half hour unable to concentrate. Her image had burned itself into his brain. She had his loins hard and aching. The woman lured him from his work like the Sirens had lured Ulysses after Troy.

He began to worry that she hadn't put on enough sunblock. Weren't there places on that long, slim body she couldn't reach?

Hardly knowing what he was about, he slammed out of his office and found himself outside, towering grimly over her. Not that she so much as bothered to glance away from her damn magazine, even though she must have heard his heavy footsteps, even though he cast a shadow over the pages.

He felt like a fool.

"You're going to burn," he growled with some annoyance.

"Do you think so? I've got lotion on, and my hat. But maybe you're right. I need to turn over for a while." She lowered her sunglasses to the tip of her nose and peered up at him saucily with bright, dark eyes.

Was she flirting with him? Damn her to hell and back if she was.

"Since you're out here, would you mind being a dear and rubbing some lotion on my back for me?"

He sank to his haunches, his excitement so profound at the thought of touching her that he didn't worry about her request for lotion on her back being illogical. Hadn't she forbidden his touch? And didn't she just say she intended to turn over onto her back?

He didn't care.

The lotion was warm from the sun, and her silky skin was even warmer as he rubbed the cream into it.

A moan of pure pleasure escaped her lips as his large palm made circular motions in the center of her back, and his heart raced at her response. He felt a visceral connection to her deep in his groin.

"You have strong hands. The lotion smells so deliciously sweet. Feels good, too," she whispered silkily, stretching like a cat as he stroked her.

"Thanks," he growled.

She rolled over and lay on her towel. Throwing him a dismissive glance, she lifted her magazine to shut him out.

"You can go now," she whispered.

Feeling stubborn and moody, he didn't budge. Only when he saw his oil rig looming off the starboard side did he arise and ask his crew to assemble their diving gear: fins, wet suits, marker floats and masks.

So much for working on the EU deal...

Later, when he and she stood on the teak diving platform at the stern of the yacht in their wet suits, she noticed nobody had thrown out an anchor.

"What if your yacht drifts while we're in the water?"

"She won't," he replied. "*Pegasus* is equipped with a sophisticated navigational system called dynamic positioning. On a day this calm she'll stay exactly where we position her. Believe me, it's much better than an anchor, which would allow her to swing back and forth."

"You plan so much that you think of everything. Does your planning and your fortune allow you to have everything you want?"

"Not quite everything," he murmured as he stared hungrily at her trim body.

Didn't she know she had changed everything?

For years, he'd been driven to avenge himself against her father, but no sooner had he been poised to seize his prize than he'd learned of Vera's illness. From that moment, his victory had begun to feel hollow.

Just when he'd wondered what new challenge could ever drive him as passionately as revenge once did, Kira had walked into his office to fight for her sister. He'd known he had to have her.

Trouble was, he was beginning to want more than he'd ever allowed himself to dream of wanting before. He wanted a life with her, a future, everything he'd told himself he could never risk having.

Kira stood on the platform watching Quinn in the water as he adjusted his mask.

"Come on in," he yelled.

She was removing her silver jewelry because he'd told her the flash of it might attract sharks.

"You know how I told you I've mainly confined my snorkeling to lakes or shallow lagoons," she began. "Well, the gulf's beginning to seem too big and too deep."

"I'll be right beside you, and Skip and Chuck are in the tender."

"I've seen all the *Jaws* movies."

"Not a good time to think about them."

She squinted, searching the vast expanse of the gulf for fins.

"Are you coming in or not?" he demanded.

Despite her doubts, she sucked in a deep breath and jumped in.

As she swam out to him, the water felt refreshingly cool.

After she got her mask on she and Quinn were soon surrounded by red snapper and amberjack. She was enjoying their cool, blue world so much that when he pointed out a giant grouper gliding by, she stared in awe instead of fear. Quinn's sure presence beside her in the water instilled in her a confidence she wouldn't have believed possible.

Snorkeling soon had her feeling weightless. It was as if she were flying in an alien world that dissolved into endless deep blue nothingness. As he'd promised, Quinn stayed beside her for nearly an hour. Enjoying herself, she forgot the vast blue darkness beneath them and what it concealed.

Just when she was starting to relax, a tiger shark zoomed out of the depths straight at Quinn. In her panic, she did exactly what she shouldn't have done. Kicking and thrashing wildly, she gulped in too much water. Choking, she yanked off her mask. As the fin vanished, Quinn ordered her to swim to the yacht.

In seconds, the fin was back, circling Quinn before diving again. Then the shark returned, dashing right at Quinn, who rammed it in the nose and made a motion with his arm for her to quit watching and start swimming. Staying behind her so he could keep his body between hers and the shark, he headed for the yacht, as well.

A tense knot of crewmen on the platform were shouting to them when she finally reached the yacht.

"Quinn," she yelled even as strong arms yanked her on board. "Quinn!" She barely heard his men shouting to him as she stood on the teak platform panting for breath. Then the dorsal fin slashed viciously right beside Quinn, and her fear mushroomed.

"Get him out! Somebody do something! Quinn! *Darling!*" she screamed.

Quinn swam in smooth, rapid strokes toward the stern. When he made it to the ladder, his crewmen sprang forward and hauled him roughly aboard, slamming him onto the teak platform.

Quinn tore off his mask. When he stood up, he turned to Kira, who took the desperate glint in his eyes as an invitation to hurl herself into his arms.

"You're as white as bleached bone," he said, gripping her tightly. "You're sure you're okay?"

The blaze of concern in his eyes and his tone mirrored her own wild fears for him.

"If you're okay, I'm okay," she whispered shakily, snuggling closer. She was so happy he was alive and unhurt.

"You're overreacting. It would take more than one little shark—"

"Don't joke! He could have torn off your arm!"

"He was probably just curious."

"Curious! I saw the movies, remember?"

He stared down at her in a way that made her skin heat. "In a funny way I feel indebted to the shark. Because of him, you called me darling."

"Did not!"

"Did, too," he drawled in that low tone that mesmerized her.

When she wrenched free of him, he laughed. "Okay. It must have been wishful thinking on a doomed man's part. Guess it was Chuck who let out the *d*-word."

She bit her lip to keep from smiling.

After they dressed, they met on the upper deck where they'd had breakfast earlier. Quinn wore jeans and a blue Hawaiian shirt that made his eyes seem as brilliant as the dazzling sky.

He ordered pineapple and mangoes and coffee. She was still so glad he was alive and had all his body parts she couldn't take her eyes off him.

"I have an idea," she said. "I mean…if we're looking for a less exciting adventure."

"What?"

"I could show you Murray Island."

"Where is it?"

"South of Galveston. Since I don't know where we are, I can't tell you how to get there. But it's on all the charts."

He picked up a phone and talked to his captain. When he hung up, he said, "Apparently, we're about forty nautical miles from your island. The captain says we could run into some weather, but if you want to go there, we will."

"What's a raindrop or two compared to being lunch for Jaws?"

"I love your vivid imagination."

In little over an hour, *Pegasus* was positioned off the shore of Murray Island, and Kira and Quinn were climbing down into the tender together. After Quinn revved the outboard, they sped toward the breaking surf, making for the pass between the barrier islands and the tiny harbor on the island's leeward side.

The bouncy ride beneath thickening gray storm clouds was wet and choppy. Heedless of the iffy weather, she stared ahead, laughing as the spray hit them. Quinn's eyes never strayed from his course—except when they veered to her face, which secretly thrilled her. She knew she shouldn't crave his attention so much, but ever since the shark incident, her emotions refused to behave sensibly.

He's alive. I have this moment with him. It's our honeymoon. Why not enjoy it? Why not share this island sanctuary I love with him?

Ten

Quinn watched his beachcombing bride much too avidly for his liking. He hated feeling so powerfully attracted to her. It was incomprehensible. She was Earl's daughter, a woman he barely knew, a wife who wouldn't even share his bed.

She'd slept with him once and then she'd left him, causing a pain too similar to what he'd felt after his father's death. The tenderness he continued to feel for her put him on dangerous ground, but still she possessed him in a way no other woman ever had.

It was the shark. Before they'd snorkeled, he'd been able to tell himself that he was under a temporary spell, that he could vanquish his burning need for her simply by staying out of her bed.

But he'd been afraid for her when she'd been swimming for the boat, more afraid than he'd ever been in his life.

Then he'd seen her bone-white face and the wild terror in her eyes when she'd imagined him in danger.

Once he'd been safely on board, her slim face had become luminous with joy. She'd hurled herself into his arms so violently she'd all but knocked them both back into the water again.

Nobody had ever looked at him like that.

Surely his father had loved him more, but she was here, and so beautiful, and so alive, and his—if only he could win her.

The prevailing southeasterly wind, cooler now because of the dark gray clouds, licked the crests of the waves into a foaming fury and sent her dark chestnut hair streaming back from her face as she scampered at the surf's edge. Every few steps, she knelt, not caring if a wave splashed her toes. Crouching, she examined the beach debris: tangles of seaweed, driftwood and shells.

Her long slim feet were bare, her toenails unpolished. Flip-flops dangled from her left hand.

For twenty years, his determination to succeed and get revenge had made time seem too valuable for him to waste on a beach with a woman. Most nights he'd worked, and most mornings, he'd left for his office before dawn. Driven by his dark goals, he'd often worked through entire weekends and holidays. His main sources of relaxation had been the gym or a willing woman and a glass of scotch before he hit his bed or desk again. He'd been more machine than human.

But that was before Kira.

Memories, long suppressed, stirred. As a child, he'd looked forward to the hour when his father's key would turn in the lock and he'd holler Quinn's name.

Quinn would race into his father's arms. After hugging him close, his father would lift him so high in the air

Quinn could touch the ceiling. So high, he'd felt as if he was flying. Then his dad would set him down and ruffle his hair and ask him about his day.

Never had his father been too tired to pass a football around the yard or take him to the park to chase geese. His father had helped with Quinn's homework, helped him build models, played endless games with him. His mother, on the other hand, had always been too busy to play. Then his father had died, and Quinn had known grief and loneliness.

For the first time, while indulging in this simple walk on the beach with Kira, Quinn felt a glimmer of the warmth that had lit his life before his father's death.

His father would want him to stop grieving, he realized. He'd want him to choose life, to choose the future.

Kira didn't realize she was beautiful, or that her lack of pretention and artifice made her even more attractive. Her every movement was graceful and natural. On the beach, she seemed a lovely wild thing running free.

This island was her refuge. For however long they were together, he would have to accept her world if he wanted her to accept his. No doubt, she would need to come here again from time to time.

He frowned, not liking the thought of her leaving him to stay out here all alone. Anyone could beach a small boat or tie up at her dock. Jim, the island's caretaker, had the faraway look of a man who'd checked out of life a long time ago. Quinn wasn't about to trust a dropout like him as her protector. No, he would have to get his security team to figure out how to make her safe here without intruding on her privacy. She was a free spirit, and Quinn wanted her to be happy, the way she was now, but safe, as well.

The sky was rapidly darkening from gray to black. Not that Kira seemed concerned about the gathering storm as she leaned down and picked up a shell. When she twisted, their gazes met. At her enchanting smile, his heart brimmed with way too much emotion. Then she ran over to show him her newfound treasure. When she held it up, her eyes shone, and the tiny window that had opened into his soul widened even further.

"Look, it's a lightning whelk," she cried.

"It's huge," he said, turning the cone-shaped shell over in his hand to properly admire it.

"At least a foot long. I've never seen one so big. And it's in perfect condition. Did you know it's the state shell of Texas?"

Shaking his head, he shot a glance at the darkening sky before he handed it back to her. "Do you collect shells?"

"Not really, but I'd like to give you this one. So you can remember Murray Island."

And *her,* he thought. "As if I could ever forget," he said. "I'll cherish it."

"I'm sure." She attempted a laugh and failed. "A new gem for your art collection."

"It's already my favorite thing."

Stronger now, the wind whipped her hair, and the sand bit into his legs.

"We should take cover," he said. "Storm's coming in. Fast. I think we'd better make a run for the house!"

"I'll race you!" Giggling as she danced on her toes, she sprinted toward the house, and because he liked watching her cute butt when she ran, he held back and let her win.

Darting from room to room as the wind howled and the frame structure shuddered, she gave him a quick tour of the house. A shady front porch looked out onto the raging gulf. Two bedrooms, a bath and a kitchen were connected by screened breezeways to each other and to the porch.

The southern bedroom had a wall of windows. "This is my favorite room," she said. "There's always a breeze, so I usually sleep here."

When she cracked a window, the room cooled instantly as storm gusts swept through it.

Deliberately, he stared outside at the rain instead of at her narrow bed. Since it was much too easy to imagine her long, lithe body on that mattress beneath him, he concentrated on the fat raindrops splatting on sand.

"With all the doors and windows open, the prevailing breezes cool the house on the hottest summer days," she said.

"If you open everything up, doesn't that make you vulnerable to a break-in?"

"No one usually comes here except me and Jim."

All anybody had to do was slit a screen to get inside. She would be defenseless. If Quinn had known how vulnerable she was while she'd been gone, he would have been even crazier with worry.

"Would you like some tea?" she said. "While we wait out the weather?"

"Sure."

When he nodded, she disappeared into the kitchen, leaving him to explore the room. A violent gust hit the house as the storm broke with full force. Somewhere, a breezeway door slammed so hard the entire house shook. Then papers fluttered under her bed. Curious, he knelt and pulled them out.

To his amazement, he discovered dozens of watercolors, all of himself, all ripped in two. He was trying to shove the entire collection back under the bed, when he heard her light footsteps at the doorway.

"Oh, my God," she said. "I forgot about those. Don't think... I mean... They don't mean anything!"

"Right."

You just painted picture after picture of me with violent, vivid brushstrokes. Then you shredded them all. For no reason.

"You obviously weren't too happy with me," he muttered.

"I really don't want to talk about it."

"Did you paint anything else...besides me?"

"A few birds."

"How many?"

"Not so many. One actually." She turned away as if uncomfortable with that admission.

Obviously, she was just as uneasy about her feelings for him as he was about his obsession with her.

"Why don't we drink our tea and go back to the yacht," he said brusquely.

"Fine with me."

"I shouldn't have pulled those pictures out," he said.

"We said we were going to forget about them."

"Right. We did." So, while he'd been obsessing about her absence, maybe she'd done a bit of obsessing herself. He took a long breath.

They sat on the porch drinking tea as the gray fury of the storm lashed the island. Now that he wanted to leave, the weather wasn't cooperating. To the contrary. Monstrous black waves thundered against the beach while rain drummed endlessly against the metal roof. No way could he trust his small tender in such high seas.

"Looks like we're stuck here for the duration," he said. So much for distracting himself from his bride anytime soon.

She nodded, her expression equally grim. "Sorry I suggested coming here."

The squalls continued into the night, so for supper she

heated a can of beans and opened cans of peaches and to-matoes. Happily, she produced a bottle of scotch that she said she kept hidden.

"We have to hide liquor from the pirates," she told him with a shy smile.

"Pirates?" he asked.

"We call anyone who lands on the island pirates. We leave the house open so they don't have to break in. Because they will if we don't."

"So, you're not entirely unaware of the dangers of being here all alone?"

"Jim's here."

"Right. Jim."

Quinn poured himself a drink and toasted good old Jim. Then he poured another. When he'd drained the second, she began to glow. Her smile and eyes looked so fresh and sparkly, he saw the danger of more liquor and suggested they go to bed.

"Separate bedrooms, of course," he said, "since that's what you want."

Nodding primly, she arose and led him to the guest bed-room. When she left him, he stripped off his shirt and lay down. She wouldn't leave his thoughts. He remembered her brilliant eyes lighting up when she saw him hauled safely onto *Pegasus*. He remembered how shyly she'd blushed every time she'd looked at him in his office, when she'd faced him down to ask him not to marry her sister. He remembered her breasts in the skimpy T-shirt she'd worn today and her cute butt and long legs in her white shorts as she'd raced him across the deep sand back to the house.

With the scotch still causing visions of her to warm his blood, he couldn't sleep for thinking of her on her narrow bed in the next room. Would she sleep curled in a ball like a child or stretched out like a woman? Was she naked? Or in her bra and panties? Did she desire him, too?

Remembering all the things she'd done to him in his loft in San Antonio, he began to fantasize that she was in the bed with him, her long legs tangled with his. That got him even hotter.

If only they were on board the yacht so he could hide out in his office on the upper deck and bury himself in paperwork. Here, there was nothing to think about but her lying in the bed next door.

At some point, he managed to fall asleep only to dream of her. In his dream, she slipped as lightly as a shadow into his bedroom. Slim, teasing fingers pulled back his sheet. Then, calling his name in husky, velvet tones, she slid into bed beside him. Her eyes blazed with the same fierce passion he'd seen when she'd realized he was safely back on board the yacht, away from the shark's teeth.

His heart constricted. Was this love? If it wasn't, it felt too dangerously close to the emotion for comfort. Even in his dream he recoiled from that dark emotion. Love had ruined his life and the life of his father. Hadn't it?

Then, in the dream, she kissed him, her sensual mouth and tongue running wildly over his lips and body while her hands moved between his legs and began to stroke. Soon he forgot about the danger of love and lost all power to resist her.

Lightning crashed, startling him. When his eyes flew open he heard the roar of the surf. He was alone in a strange, dark bedroom with sweat dripping from his long, lean body onto damp sheets, aching all over because he wanted to make love to his forbidden wife.

She was driving him crazy. On a low, frustrated groan, he hurled himself out of bed and stalked onto the breezeway in the hope that the chill, damp wind whipping through the screens would cool his feverish body and restore his sanity.

"Quinn!" came Kira's soft, startled cry, the sexy sound setting his testosterone-charged nerves on high alert.

He whirled to face her just as a bolt of lightning flashed. Her hair streaming in the wind, she leaned against a post some ten feet away, in the shadows. Momentarily blinded from the lightning, he couldn't make her out in the darkness. Imagining the rest of her, his blood notched a degree hotter.

"You'd better get back to your room," he rasped.

"What's the use when I couldn't sleep even if I did? Storms like this are exciting, aren't they?"

"Just do as I said and go."

"This is my house. Why should I do what you say, if I prefer watching the storm...and you?" she said in a low, breathless tone.

"Because if you plan to keep me in a separate bedroom, it's the smart thing to do."

"Used to giving orders, aren't you? Well, I'm not used to taking them. Since I'm your wife, maybe it's time I taught you that. I could teach you a lot..."

Thunder rolled, and rain slashed through the breezeway furiously, sending rivulets of water across the concrete floor.

"Go," he muttered.

"Maybe I will." But her husky laughter defied him. "Then, maybe not."

When she turned, instead of heading across the breezeway toward her bedroom, she unlatched a screen door behind her and ran onto the beach. As she did, a blaze of white fire screamed from the wet black sky to the beach.

Hell! She was going to get herself fried if he didn't bring her back.

"Kira!" he yelled after her.

When she kept running, he heaved himself after her, his bare feet sinking deeply into the soft, wet sand and crushed shells as he sprinted. Sheets of rain soaked him through within seconds.

She didn't get more than twenty feet before he caught her by the waist and pulled her roughly into his arms. She was wet and breathless, her long hair glued to her face, her T-shirt clinging to her erect nipples.

Quinn closed his eyes and willed himself to think of something besides her breasts and the light in her eyes. But as the cold rain pounded him, her soft warmth and beauty and the sweetness of her scent drew him. He opened his eyes and stared down at her. Slowly, she put her arms around him and looked at him as she had in his dreams, with her heart shining in her eyes.

Laughing, she said, "Have you ever seen anything so wild? Don't you love it?"

He hadn't deliberately stood in the rain or stomped in a puddle since he'd been a kid, when his dad had encouraged him to be a boy, as he'd put it. Hell, maybe that was his loss. Maybe it wasn't right for him to control himself so tightly.

As the torrents washed them, he picked her up and spun her crazily, high above his head. Then he lowered her, slowly, oh, so slowly. He let her breasts and tummy and thighs slide against his body, which became even harder in response to hers.

If only she'd stop looking at him with such fire in her eyes… She made him crave a different kind of life…. One of brightness, warmth and love.

"Kiss me," she whispered, pressing herself into his rock-hard thighs, smiling wantonly up at him when she felt his impressive erection.

So—she wanted him, too.

Kissing her so hard she gasped, he plunged his tongue into her mouth. The rain streamed over their fused bodies and the lightning flashed and the thunder rolled. He knew he should take her inside, but she tasted so good that, for the life of him, he couldn't let her go.

He would regret this, he was sure. But later. Not now, when she smelled of rain. Not when the wild surf roared on all sides of them. Not when his blood roared even louder.

Tonight, he had to have her.

Eleven

When he stripped her and laid her on the bed, she closed her eyes. With her face softly lit by an expectant smile and her damp hair fanning darkly across her pillow, she looked too lovely and precious for words.

"I wanted you to come to me… Even before…you appeared in the breezeway," she admitted, blushing shyly. "I know I shouldn't have…but I just lay on my bed craving you."

"Imagine that. We're on the same page for once."

"I don't want to want you…"

"I know exactly how you feel."

Thank God, he'd thought to stuff some condoms into his wallet before they'd left the yacht—just in case. Thinking about them now made him remember the first time—the one time he'd failed to protect her—and the little clock ticking in the back of his mind ticked a little louder.

She could be pregnant.

Part of him hoped she *was* pregnant...with a son. His son... No, *their* son. A little boy with dark hair who he could play ball with as his father had played with him. They would call him Kade. Quinn would come home, call his name, and the boy would come running.

Foolish dream.

Stripping off his wet jeans and Jockey shorts, he pulled the condoms out of his wallet and laid them on the bedside table. Still thinking she could very well be pregnant and that he wouldn't mind nearly as much as he should, he stroked the creaminess of her cheek with his thumb. When her eyes sparked with anticipation, he kissed each eyelid and then her smiling mouth.

"Such tiny wrists," he said as he lifted them to his lips. He let his warm breath whisper across her soft skin. "Your heart is beating faster than a rabbit's. So, you did want me...my darlin'. Feed my bruised ego—admit it."

She laughed helplessly. "Okay—I'm tingling in so many places, I feel weak enough to faint."

He touched her breasts, her slender waist, the thatch of silken curls where her thighs were joined. He pressed his lips to all those secret places so reverently that his kisses transcended the physical.

"Better." He smiled. "I told you that you'd change your mind about sex." Triumphantly, he skimmed his mouth along her jawline. With each kiss that he bestowed, she claimed another piece of his heart.

"That you did. Are you always right? Is that how you became so rich?"

He kissed her earlobe, chuckling when she shivered in response.

"Focus is the key in so many endeavors. It only took a day, and I didn't once try to seduce you, now, did I?"

"Stop crowing like a rooster who's conquered a henhouse! I see you brought plenty of protection…which means you intended this to happen."

"I was hopeful. I usually feel optimistic about achieving my goals." He trailed the tip of his tongue along her collarbone.

She moved restlessly beneath him. "You're rubbing it in, and I said don't gloat." When he licked her earlobe again, she shuddered, causing a blazing rush of fire to sizzle through him. "Just do it," she begged.

"Why are you always in such a hurry, sweet Kira?"

Because she was unable to take her eyes from his face, she blew out a breath. Except for clenching her fingers and pressing her lips together, she lay still, as if fighting for patience.

"After all," he continued, "for all practical purposes, this is our wedding night."

Her quick scowl made him wonder why the hell he'd reminded them both of the marriage he'd forced her into.

Before she could protest, he kissed her lips. Soon her breathing was deep and ragged, and it wasn't long until she was quivering beneath his lips and begging him for more.

Her hands moved over his chest and then lower, down his torso and dipping lower still. When her fingers finally curled firmly around the swollen length of his shaft, he shuddered. Soon she had him as hot and eager to hurry as she was. He was out of control, completely in her thrall.

"I bet we're on the same page now," she said huskily, a triumphant lilt in her husky tone.

"Sexy, wanton witch." Unwrapping a condom, he sheathed himself.

Compelled to claim her as his, he plunged into tight, satiny warmth. Stomach to stomach. Thigh to thigh. The moment he was inside her, she wrapped her legs around his waist and urged him even deeper.

"Yes," she whispered as a tortured moan was torn from her lips.

"Yes," he growled, holding her even closer.

Then, some force began to build as he stroked in and out of her, his rhythm growing as hard and steady as the surf dancing rhythmically against the shore. His blood heated; his heart drummed faster. When he fought to slow down, she clung tighter, writhing, begging, urging him not to stop—shattering what was left of his fragile control.

With a savage cry, he climaxed. She felt so good, so soft, so delectable. Grabbing her bottom, he ground himself into her, plunging deeper. As she arched against him, he spilled himself inside her.

She went wild, trembling, screaming his name, and her excitement sent him over the fatal edge he'd vowed never to cross. Walls inside him tumbled. He didn't want to feel like this—not toward her, not toward any woman.

But he did.

Long minutes after he rolled off her, he lay beside her, fighting for breath and control.

"Wow," she said.

Even though sex had never felt so intense before, he didn't trust his feelings. Why give her any more power than she already had by admitting them? But though he confessed nothing, her sweet warmth invaded him, soothing all the broken parts of his soul.

She sidled closer and touched his lips with feverish fingertips, her eyes alight with sensual invitation. As she stroked his mouth and cheek teasingly, desire sizzled through him. He was rock-hard in another instant.

No way in hell would one time suffice. For either of them. With one sure, swift movement, he slid nearer so that his sex touched hers. When she stared up at him hungrily, he kissed her brow, her eyelids and then the tip of her pert nose. Then he edged lower, kissing her breasts and navel. Spreading her legs, he went all the way down, laving those sweet forbidden lips that opened to him like the silken petals of a warm flower. The tip of his tongue flicked inside, causing her to moan.

"Darlin'," he said softly. "You're perfect."

"I want you inside me. So much."

He wanted that, too, so he eased into her, gently this time, and held her tight against him. How could she feel so wonderful in his arms? So right? Like she belonged there, always, till the end of time? How could this be? She was Earl's daughter, a woman he'd coerced into marriage.

"How can this be?" she asked, her words mirroring his dark thoughts.

He took his time, and when it ended in violent, bitter-sweet waves of mutual passion, he felt again the inexplicable peace that left no space for hate or thoughts of revenge. He simply wanted her, wanted to be with her. He didn't want to hurt anything or anybody she loved.

"You're dangerously addictive," he whispered against her earlobe.

Her sweet face was flushed; her lips bruised and swollen from his kisses.

"So are you," she said with a tremulous smile even as her wary eyes reminded him that she hadn't married him for this. "This wasn't supposed to happen, was it? You didn't want this connection any more than I did."

"No..." His mood darkened as he remembered she didn't believe this was a real marriage.

His old doubts hit him with sweeping force. Tomorrow... if it would make her happy, he'd swear to her he'd never touch her again. But not tonight. Tonight, he had to hold her close, breathe in her scent, lose himself in her...dream of a different kind of life with her.

Just for tonight she was completely his.

Hugging him close, she sighed and fell asleep. Beside her, he lay awake for hours watching her beautiful face in the dark, longing and…wishing for the impossible.

When Kira awoke, her arms and legs were tangled around Quinn's. She'd slept so well. For a fleeting instant she felt happy just to be with him.

Last night he'd made her feel precious and adored. Until…the end. With a frown, she remembered how tense and uncertain he'd seemed right before he'd crushed her close and she'd fallen asleep in his arms.

How could she have thrown herself at him? Begged him? He was determined never to love again. Sex, even great sex, would not change his mind.

Despite regrets and misgivings, the gray morning was beautiful. Rain was falling softly, scenting the island with its freshness. A gentle breeze whirred in the eaves while dazzling sunlight splashed the far wall with vivid white.

Had she been sure of Quinn's love, it would have felt romantic to be nestled so warmly in his strong arms. She would have reveled in the sensual heat created by his breath stirring her hair.

But wrapped in cocoonlike warmth with him when she knew he couldn't ever care for her only aroused longings for forbidden things like friendship and affection.

He was going to break her heart. She knew it.

Slowly, she shifted to her side of the bed. Careful not to wake him, she eased herself to her feet. When he smiled in his sleep, she couldn't help thinking him the most stunningly handsome man she'd ever seen.

He looked so relaxed. So peaceful. Last night, he'd taken great care to make her happy in bed. Longing to brush his thick hair away from his brow filled her. Because of what they'd shared, she simply wanted to touch him.

No... She had to remember his experience. He was probably just a great lover and had taken no special pains with her.

Fearing she'd accidentally awaken him if she didn't stop gaping at his virile, male beauty, she tiptoed onto the breezeway where salty air assaulted her. When her tummy flipped violently, causing a brief dizzy spell, she sank against the doorjamb.

After a deep breath, the dizziness loosened its hold. She wasn't sick exactly, but her face felt clammy and she was queasy in a way she'd never been before.

Alarmed, she swallowed. Shakily, she smoothed her damp hair back from her face.

Again, she remembered that Quinn hadn't used a condom their first time in bed. In her head, she began to count the days since her last period, which she already knew was a little late. It was time...past time...for her period to start...and under the circumstances, her odd light-headedness made her anxious.

What if she were pregnant? How would Quinn react? He had not married her because he loved her or wanted a family. Quite the opposite. He'd used protection every single time since that first lapse. She'd never want to force him to stay married to her because of a baby. She wanted love, acceptance. Making their marriage of convenience a permanent situation was the best way to guarantee she'd never find it.

Quickly, she said a little prayer and decided not to borrow trouble just yet. Why upset him until she knew for sure? Still, no matter how she denied it, a seed of worry had taken root.

By the time Quinn had awakened, yanked on his jeans

and called for her, Kira had had her first cup of coffee and felt almost calm enough to face him. As she sat on the front porch, she watched the last gusts of the storm whip the high waves into a frenzy and hurl them against the shore.

At the sound of his approaching footsteps her belly tightened. Then she reminded herself there had only been one lapse…so there really wasn't much danger of pregnancy, was there?

"Kira?"

Concentrating on the angry seas, she wondered how soon the waves would calm down enough for them to leave. When she heard Quinn turning away from the porch, maybe because she hadn't answered, and stomping around somewhere inside the kitchen calling her name, she sensed he was out of sorts, too.

The door behind her creaked.

"Why didn't you answer when I called you?" His low voice was harsh, uncertain. "Avoiding me, are you?"

She didn't turn around to look at him. "Maybe I didn't hear you."

"Maybe you did."

"The seas are still so high, it may be a while before we can leave," she said.

"I see. After last night, you're too embarrassed to talk about anything but the weather. Are you blaming me because I didn't stick to our no-sex deal?"

Hot color climbed her cheeks. "No. I know that what happened was as much my fault as yours."

"But you don't like it."

"Look, what I don't like is being bullied into this marriage in the first place."

"Right."

"If you hadn't forced me to marry you, we wouldn't be

trapped on this island together. Then last night wouldn't have happened."

"Okay, then. So, am I to assume from your mutinous expression that you want to go back to our no-sex deal?"

Why were men always so maddeningly literal? All she wanted was a little reassurance. Instead, he'd launched into the blame game.

Well, she wasn't about to admit she'd craved him last night or that she'd enjoyed everything they'd done together. Nor would she admit that despite everything, she still wanted him. That the last thing she wanted was their no-sex deal. To admit any of that would prove her irrational and give him too much power over her.

When she sat staring at the stormy gulf in silence, he squared his shoulders. "It's too bad the waters are so rough and you're stuck with me, but if we've waited it out this long, I don't intend to push our luck by trying to take the tender out when we could capsize. I'm hungry. Do you want to share that last can of pork and beans with me for breakfast or not?"

The mere thought of canned pork and beans made her mouth go dry and her tummy flip. Within seconds, she began to perspire.

"Or not," she whispered, shaking her head fiercely as she inhaled a deep breath to settle her stomach.

"Are you all right? You look a little pale," he said, stepping closer. "Sick almost."

"I'm fine," she snapped, turning away so he couldn't read her face.

"I wasn't too rough last night, was I?" he asked, the genuine concern in his low tone touching her.

"The less said about what happened the better!"

With a weary look, he nodded. "I talked to my captain via satellite phone. *Pegasus* held up well under the rough seas and squalls. The crew had a bit of a bad night, but other than a case or two of seasickness, all is well."

"I'm glad."

"Look, for what it's worth, I'm sorry I reneged on our bargain and made love to you."

She knotted her hands and unknotted them.

"I took advantage."

"No, you didn't! I was the one who ran out in the storm and lured you after me!" She jumped up. Hugging herself, she walked over to the window. "I'm sure any man would have done the same."

"Look, I'm not just some guy you picked up off the street who is out to get what he can get."

She whirled on him. "Whatever you may think because of that night we shared in San Antonio, I don't do one-night stands, either!"

"I know that. I believe that. I wouldn't have married you otherwise."

"I wonder. Did anything besides my last name really matter to you?"

His face went cold. "I'm your husband. Last night I knew what you wanted and what you didn't want. But in the end, it didn't matter."

"You told me you'd have me in your bed in no time, and you did. So why don't you chalk up another win for your side in your little plan to get revenge against my father."

"Damn it. Because that's not how I feel about it! Or about you!"

"Don't romanticize what happened! We were bored and trapped. Big deal. It's over."

"The hell it is."

"Ours is only a marriage of convenience."

"Do you have to constantly remind me of that?"

"Why not, if it's the truth?"

"Is it? Does it have to be?"

"Yes! Yes!"

He was silent for a long moment. "If that's really how you feel, I won't sleep with you again. You can have your marriage of convenience—permanently. I hope it makes you happy!"

His cold announcement chilled her. Not that she was about to let him see how hurt she felt.

"Great! Now that that's settled, go! Eat your beans and leave me alone!"

"All right. And after I eat them, I'm going out. For a walk. To check on the tender. And I won't be back till the storm's over."

"Great! Perfect!"

When he slammed out of the porch and stalked toward the kitchen, her stomach twisted sharply. She felt ill, really ill. Clutching her stomach, she ran out the back door so he wouldn't see, knelt on the damp sand in the lightly falling rain, and was sick.

She *was* pregnant. She just knew she was.

His strides long and quick because he was anxious to get as far from the house—and from her—as fast as he could, Quinn stalked down the beach toward the dock. As his heels thudded into the deep sand, his head pounded viciously. Their quarrel had given him the headache from hell.

How different he felt now than he had when he'd first woken up. The air had smelled so fresh. He'd lain in bed, his eyes closed, drinking in a contentment he hadn't known in years. Then, he'd reached for her and discovered cool sheets instead of her warm, silky body, and some part of him had gone cold.

He didn't regret his harsh words because she'd smashed

his heart. He didn't regret the sex, either. She'd been sweet, and she'd felt too good—so good that just thinking of her naked and writhing in his arms, her shining eyes big as she'd begged for more had him brick-hard all over again.

When he saw the dock up ahead and the tender riding the waves, he felt intense relief.

He wasn't used to second-guessing himself or feeling the slightest guilt or confusion after sex. In his whole life he'd never awakened beside a woman who hadn't wanted him. Quite the opposite. They always clung, wanting more than he could give. Then he'd be the one to pull away. With her, he felt different. That's probably why he'd been fool enough to marry her.

From the moment Kira had shown up in his office to beg him not to marry her sister, he'd changed all the rules he'd lived by for so long. She'd tangled his emotions into a painful knot.

For some insane, ridiculous reason, he wanted to please her. He'd actually hoped she'd be happier with him after last night, so her obvious misery this morning ate at him all the more.

In his frustration, he broke into a jog. His marriage be damned. The sooner he ended this farce of a honeymoon and got back to business the better.

From now on, their marriage would be as she wished— all for show. He'd ignore the hell out of her except when there were in public.

When he reached the dock, he grabbed the stern line. After snugging the tender closer, he sprang on board.

Crafted of teak for the turbulent waters of the North Sea, she was an efficient, self-bailing craft. Maybe that was why she hadn't sunk. Also, the dock was on the leeward side of the island and in a well-protected cove.

He started the engine and smiled grimly when it purred

to life. Once he made sure the tender was sound, he shut it off, sat down and let the wind buffet him.

In no mood to return to the house or to his wife, he kept an eye on the distant horizon. As soon as the seas calmed, he'd take his bride home and get back to work. He'd lose himself in negotiations with the European Union and forget all about Kira.

His marriage was turning out to be the last thing from convenient, whatever Kira might say to the contrary.

Twelve

Quinn spoke to her as little as possible now.

If Kira had wondered how long Quinn would pretend to be interested in her, she had her answer and was miserable as a result.

No sooner had they returned to San Antonio than he'd made it clear he intended to live as he had before his marriage—working nearly every waking hour.

"The EU deal is going to command my full attention, so I won't be around much for a while," he'd said.

"Fine. I understand."

"Jason will come promptly at ten every morning to take care of you and the house."

"Jason?"

"My houseman. He's at your command. You'll find him highly competent."

Quinn had ensconced her in his fabulous loft apartment, and yes, he'd given her the master bedroom. Now she slept alone in the vast bed they'd shared that first night. As for himself, their first evening home, he'd packed a suitcase and moved his things into a second bedroom. Then he'd politely bid her a terse good-night, gone to bed early and left for work the next morning hours before she'd woken up.

That first morning Jason, a much older man, who was thin-lipped and skeletal, had greeted her so haughtily in the kitchen, she'd felt she was invading his territory.

"I'm Jason," he'd said with a vague sneer in his upper-class tone. "I'm here for whatever you need, cleaning, shopping, cooking—anything. It is my duty and privilege to please you, madam."

Madam?

"Wow! I'm really not used to being waited on. I can't think of a thing for you to do. I mean, I can pour my own cereal out of a box, can't I?"

"Cereal?" He scowled briefly. "Would you prefer an omelet?" he'd suggested with a contemptuous lift of his brows.

"Well, why not," she'd whispered, sensing they were getting off to a bad start. She wanted to be agreeable, yet she despised herself for giving in to him when he was supposed to be serving her. The man made her feel more out of place in Quinn's home than she'd felt before.

Jason had cooked a very good ham-and-vegetable omelet, and she'd dutifully eaten it. Then she'd rushed off to Betty's restaurant to help out while one of the waitresses was away, and the kitchen smells had bothered her way more than usual.

The rest of the week followed the same pattern with Quinn leaving early and returning late. Jason cooked her breakfast and made her dinner, and she began to feel grateful for his presence since it meant she wasn't totally alone.

Since Quinn was gone all the time, she might hardly have noticed she was married if she hadn't missed him so much. She was on her own, as she had been before her marriage, but because her husband was a man she found exceedingly attractive, she felt rejected and constantly unsettled. If he was home behind his shut door, she thought of him every minute.

When he was gone, she felt lost. With every passing day she grew more acutely sensitive to odors, which made her increasingly worried that he'd made her pregnant. She wanted to talk to Quinn about the situation, but she dreaded the conversation, especially now that he was so intent on avoiding her.

On the eighth day of their return, when her period still hadn't started and she was queasier than ever, she called her doctor and made an appointment for the next morning. She'd agreed to take her mother to a routine chemo treatment the same afternoon.

Jaycee had called her earlier in the week, begging her to pick up their mother for her appointment as a favor because escorting her mother for treatment made Jaycee so sad.

"So, how's it going with Quinn?" Jaycee had asked after Kira agreed.

"Fine."

"Fine? Hmm? Well, they do say the first few months are an adjustment."

"I said we're fine."

"I know you don't believe this, but he cares about you. He wanted to marry you."

"Right."

"He bought you that beautiful wedding dress, and you should have seen him when you were gone and nobody knew where you were."

"Well, he's ignoring me now," Kira confided.

"Did you two have a fight?"

She didn't answer.

"If you did, and I think you did, you need to find a way to kiss and make up."

"Why bother to make up, if we have no future?"

Kira changed the subject to her cat, Rudy, and asked if Jaycee minded keeping him a while longer. "I don't want him attaching himself to Quinn...if we're just going to break up."

"He's only a cat."

"Rudy's sensitive."

"And Quinn's not? If I were you, I'd worry more about your husband."

She was; she just wasn't going to admit it.

When Jaycee hung up, Kira had marked her mother's appointment on her calendar. She was glad to have something other than Quinn and her possible pregnancy to concentrate on.

Hours later, she was in bed that night with her light out when she heard Quinn at the door. Throwing off her covers, she started to go out and greet him. Then, pride made her stay where she was.

Wishing he'd knock on her door, she counted his approaching footsteps as he walked across the great room before he made his way down the hall.

When he paused at her door her heart beat very fast. But after a minute, he resumed walking to his own bedroom.

When his door slammed, a strangled sob rose in her throat. With a little cry, she got out of bed and ran to her window. Staring out at the brilliant city, she imagined other married couples, happier couples, slipping into bed together, snuggling close, talking about their day or their children, taking such blissful marital pleasures for granted.

Suddenly, Kira felt as lonely as a butterfly trapped in a child's glass jar.

Pulling on her robe, she wandered out into the great room. Baby or not, she could not live like this, with a husband who didn't want her.

Behind her, she heard a floorboard creak. Whirling, she caught her breath at the sight of Quinn standing barechested in the dark. His shadowed eyes looked haunted.

"You okay?" His low, harsh voice made her shiver. She wanted to be held, loved and crushed against him.

"I'm fine. And you?"

"A little tired, but the deal with the EU seems to be coming together. I'll be going to London for a few days."

"Oh."

"A car's coming for me at 5:00 a.m. Don't worry. I'll be careful so as not to wake you."

How could he be so obtuse? Was he just indifferent? Or was he still angry with her for their harsh exchange on the island?

She wanted to scream at him that he should kiss her goodbye properly. She wanted to drive him to the airport herself. But she kept such foolish thoughts to herself, and he only stared at her from the dark with his intense, burning gaze. She thought he was watching her, waiting—but for what?

Jaycee had advised her to kiss and make up. But how? To what purpose, when he so clearly had his mind on more important things?

After a few minutes of staring at each other in stony silence, he said good-night.

The next morning, when she heard the front door close behind him, she got up. Throwing away all pride, she rushed from her room into the foyer that was filled with crimson light, managing to catch up to him as he waited for the elevator.

"Sorry to wake you," he murmured, concern in his eyes.

"Don't be. I had to say goodbye and wish you a safe journey, didn't I," she whispered, surprised that she could sound so calm, so normal when she felt so incredibly depressed. "I'll miss you."

His dark brows arched warily. "Will you now?"

"I will," she said.

After another long moment spent considering her, he sighed and drew her close against his long, hard body. "I'll miss you, too." He paused. "Sorry about the last week or so."

"I'm sorry, too."

"Habib will call you later and give you all the numbers where I can be reached. I'll think of you in London. I really will miss you. You know that, don't you?" he murmured.

Would he really?

Wrapping her closer, he kissed her hard. She clung to him, probably revealing more of her real feelings than was wise. Then the elevator pinged, and he was forced to let her go or be late. Holding her gaze, he picked up his suitcase and strode through the doors.

She couldn't turn away or stop looking at him or take even one step toward the loft until the door shut.

Pregnant! Needing a moment to take in that news, Kira clenched the steering wheel of her Toyota as she sat in the parking lot of the medical complex and kneaded her forehead with her knuckles.

After a brief exam, the doctor had ripped off his latex gloves and confirmed she was pregnant.

"How do you know? You haven't even tested me."

"When you've been doing this as long as I have, young lady, you just know."

Within minutes, a pregnancy test administered in his office confirmed his opinion.

After the office visit, she felt both numb and tingly as she sat in her car. Biting her lip, she pulled out the slip of paper where she'd written all the numbers Habib had given her earlier. After calculating the time difference between the U.K. and Texas, she grabbed her cell phone and started dialing. Then she stopped. Quinn was probably extremely busy or in an important meeting. Her news would distract him from what was all-important to him—the deal. Better to share the news with him in person when she was sure she had his full attention and could gauge his reaction.

Still, her heart felt as if it was brimming over. She was bursting to tell someone…who would be every bit as excited as she was.

Mother. Suddenly, she was very glad she would be taking her mother to treatment today. Who better to confide in than her precious baby's grandmother? Nobody adored babies, anybody's babies, more than her mother did. Her mother would be happier about this news than anyone, and goodness knew, with all she was going through, she needed a cheerful future to contemplate.

"Oh, my dear," her mother gushed, setting her flowered china teacup aside and seizing Kira's hand in both of her thin ones. Kira had waited until after her mother's treatment, when they could sit down together at Betty's, to share the news.

How weak her mother's grasp felt, even if her eyes were alight with joy.

"Such wonderful news! The best ever! Unbelievable! And it was so easy for you two! And so soon!"

A fierce rush of pride swamped Kira. Never had her mother been so pleased with her. Such rapture had always been reserved for Jaycee's accomplishments.

"Have you told Quinn yet?" her mother asked.

"I started to call him. Then I thought I'd wait...until he comes home, until he's not so distracted."

"So, I'm the first!" Her mother beamed so brightly she almost looked as she had before the illness. Her grip strengthened. "I'm going to beat this thing and live for a very long time. I have to...if I'm to see my darling grandbaby grow up."

Kira's gaze blurred, and she had to turn away to hide her emotion. She felt exhilarated and proud, and a big part of her pleasure had to do with the fact that for once she'd trumped Jaycee.

Oh, why hadn't she ever felt sure of her parents' love?

The river sparkled beside their table outside Betty's. Kira was thrilled her mother's fighting spirit was intact and that she felt reasonably strong. But most of all, she couldn't help being glad that she'd been the one to make her mother so happy.

"Your father will be just as excited as I am. He's very up on Quinn's successes in London, too. So this will be a doubly great day for him."

"Oh, so he's already heard from Quinn?" Kira whispered, feeling more than a little hurt that Quinn had called her father and not her.

"Yes, and it sounds like things are going very well," her mother replied. "Am I to assume by the way you're biting your lip that *you* haven't spoken to him?"

"He texted me, saying he'd arrived in London safely. I'm not hurt. Not in the least."

After studying her for a long moment, her mother looked

dubious. "Well, I'm sure he'll be so happy to hear your exciting news."

Would he be? Oh, how she hoped so, but her doubts soon had her biting her lower lip again.

"Don't do that, dear. How many times have I told you that biting your lip like that chaps your beautiful mouth?"

"When I was a child, Mother!"

"Well, just the same, I know you want to be beautiful for Quinn when he comes home, now, don't you?"

"Right. I do." She glanced at the muddy green river and tried to focus on a white duck. "Frankly, I'm a little worried about telling him. You know…we didn't marry under the best of circumstances."

"I wish you wouldn't make so much of that. I really think it means something when a couple gets pregnant so easily," her mother said almost enviously.

"What are you saying?"

"Sometimes it doesn't work that way… Earl and I had a terrible time getting pregnant with…with you. But let's not go there."

Did she only imagine the shadow that passed over her mother's thin face?

"Is anything wrong, Mother?"

"No, dear."

But her mother looked away and something in her manner and stiff posture rang alarm bells inside Kira. When the silence between them lengthened and grew more strained, she was sure her mother was worrying about something.

"What's wrong? Have I upset you?"

Her mother stared at her, hesitating. "I guess…it's only natural that your news would stir up the past."

"When you were pregnant with me?"

A single tear traced down her mother's cheek. "No..." She clenched her napkin.

"Did the doctor tell you something when you were alone with her that has you upset? Bad news of some kind?"

"Dear God, no!" Her mother took her hand. "No. It's not that. It's nothing like that. It's about you..." Her mother's eyes filled with some unfathomable emotion. "I was never pregnant with you."

"What?"

"I...*we* tried so hard, your father and I, to have a baby. So dreadfully hard. You know how I am. I took my temperature all the time. Ten times a day. But I didn't...I couldn't get pregnant...no matter what I did. We went to so many specialists, and they told us that it was my fault, not your father's. Some hormone imbalance. And then...we never told anyone, not even you, the truth."

"What truth?" Under the table Kira's hands fisted so tightly her nails dug bloody crescents into her palms.

"I couldn't conceive, so, in the end, we adopted."

"What?"

"You're adopted. Please don't look so upset! I could never have had a daughter of my own as wonderful as you. You've always been so sweet. Like now. Coming with me for my treatment when poor Jaycee couldn't bear it. She hates thinking of me being sick. She's too much like me, you see. I'm strong in some ways, but weak in others. Until now, I could never admit, not to anyone, that you weren't my biological child. It represented my biggest imperfection as a woman."

"Oh, my God." Kira felt overwhelmed, hollow. Suddenly she remembered all the little things that had never added up in her life. The rest of her family members were blond and blue-eyed, while she had dark eyes and hair. She was tall and slim, while her mother and Jaycee were more petite and curvy.

She'd never been as interested in style or fashion as they were. She'd been wired more emotionally and hadn't thought as logically as they did. Maybe this was why she'd always felt as if she hadn't belonged in her family. Maybe she'd always sensed this huge falsehood in her life.

"I felt like such a failure," her mother continued. "As a woman. For not being able to conceive a child. And then suddenly, inexplicably, when you were two years old, I became pregnant with Jaycee…without even trying. When she was so perfect, so gorgeous, I felt I'd achieved something grand by giving birth. But really, having you was always just as big an achievement. Only I never appreciated it until now. Illness like this can change you, make you wiser somehow.

"I was silly and so unsure when I was young. I know I haven't always understood you, but you are very precious to me."

Kira could say nothing. She was as overwhelmed as a stage actress in a drama who'd forgotten all her lines. Her mind had gone blank.

"I'm so glad you have Quinn. We all suffered so much when Kade died right after selling the company to us. Your father loved Kade like a brother. And then, all these years later, to have Quinn take over the company at the best possible moment for us was a fortunate irony. And now this baby. This wonderful baby will make everything right again. I just know it will.

"I'll get well, and you'll be happy with Quinn. You'll quit…doubting you belong together because you'll have this baby to love together. Nothing can bring a couple closer than a child."

"If only life were that simple."

"Sometimes it is."

Kira couldn't think about her adoption and what it meant right now. So she focused on finding out more about Quinn's past.

Squeezing her eyes shut, she reopened them. "Mother, why did Quinn blame Daddy for his father's death?"

"Your father and Kade Sullivan created Murray Oil. Well, back then it was Sullivan and Murray Oil. Esther Sullivan was extravagant, but Kade adored her. Of course, he was always borrowing from Earl, always needing more… because of her, you see. Esther's needs were insatiable. In time, Kade began to gamble on the side and play the market. For years he was lucky, but then one day his luck ran out.

"When money went missing at the company, from accounts he was responsible for, your father asked him some pointed questions. Kade got angry. The money was found eventually, but the misunderstanding had caused a rift between them.

"Kade said he wanted out, so Earl bought him out. But when times got better and the stock price took off, Kade got hard feelings and started drinking and bad-mouthing your father, especially to Quinn, I think. Around that time, Esther divorced Kade and took whatever he had left.

"Not too long afterward, Earl made a deal that tripled the worth of Murray Oil. Kade claimed the deal had been his idea and wanted compensation, so he sued. He lost the suit, and Quinn discovered his father's body in his shop off the garage. Supposedly Kade had been cleaning his shotgun and it went off. Accidentally. But who knows? Not that Kade ever seemed like the kind of man who'd kill himself. In fact, your father definitely believes it was an accident.

"Oh, my darling, let's not talk of such depressing things.

I much prefer to think about my future grandbaby. Do you want a boy or a girl?"

"A little boy," she whispered. "A little boy with blue eyes who looks just like Quinn and Kade."

"So, you're beginning to love him a little."

With all her heart. Yet she wasn't ready to admit that, not even to her mother.

But her mother saw the truth. "I told you so," she said triumphantly. "And no wonder. He's everything any woman with half a brain would want in a husband."

Not quite everything. He could never return her love, Kira thought.

Thirteen

Quinn remained in London for a week, during which time Kira ached for him. She didn't know how she could miss a man who'd worked so hard to ignore her before he'd left, but she did.

Then, suddenly he sent her a brief text informing her of his flight information for the next day. He said he'd hired a driver to pick him up. Then, right before he boarded his plane, he called her cell while she was still asleep. When she didn't answer, he left a message saying he'd called to remind her of a company party they were attending that evening an hour after his flight was scheduled to land.

So, there would be no private time together his first night home.

"You can call my secretary to find out what to wear," he'd said over the phone. Then his voice had lowered. "Missed you...worse than I thought I would," he'd whispered before ending the call.

Damn. Damn. Damn. What rotten luck that she'd missed his call. What else might he have said if they'd actually talked? She replayed his message several times just to hear his mesmerizing voice say he'd missed her.

A lump formed in her throat. Why had she muted her phone before laying it on her bedside table?

Dialing his secretary, she asked what she should wear to the party.

"It's formal, but Mr. Sullivan did tell me to suggest you wear something red."

"Why red?"

"He didn't say. The deal he pulled off with the EU will have far-reaching consequences for Murray Oil, hopefully positive. Since he's returning in triumph, the party's important to him. I'd suggest you go with his color choice, in case it fits with a bigger plan."

Her heart thumping wildly, Kira took off early from Betty's to indulge in a shopping spree with her mother in search of the perfect sexy red dress. Then she rushed home, with her low-cut scarlet gown and a pair of new heels, so she could take special pains getting dressed.

After the party, if Quinn was in a good mood, she would tell him she was pregnant.

At six, while she was combing her hair, his driver called to tell her Quinn's plane had just landed. "I'll have him home soon."

"Can I please talk to him?"

"He's on the phone. Business. But I'll tell him to call you as soon as he finishes."

When Quinn's key turned in the lock, Kira hurried to the door to greet him. His luggage thumped heavily on the floor. Then he strode through the foyer with his phone still pressed to his ear.

His voice rang with authority as he stepped into the living room. When she met his hard, dark eyes, she saw the shadows of weariness under them. Even if he hadn't bothered to call her from the car, she was so thrilled he was home, her heart leaped with pure joy.

"Gotta go," he said abruptly. "We'll wrap this up in the morning." He flipped his phone shut and stared at her. "Sorry about the phone call. Business."

"Of course. I understand." She smiled tremulously.

His mouth curved, but his smile played out before it reached his eyes.

She wanted to rush into his arms, and it was only with great effort that she remained where she was. No matter how eager she felt, she would not throw herself at him.

"You look pale," he said. "Thinner. Are you okay?"

She hadn't been eating as regularly due to her morning sickness, but she couldn't tell him that. At least, not now.

"I'm fine," she whispered.

"Right. Why is that answer always your first line of defense?"

She didn't know what to say to him. If only he would take her in his arms and kiss her, maybe that would break down the barriers between them.

His eyes burned her, and his hands were clenched. Was being married to her so difficult for him?

"I like the dress. It becomes you," he murmured.

She blushed, pleased.

"I bought you something." He tossed a box onto the sofa carelessly. "Open it and see if you like it." He spoke casually, as if the gift was a token and nothing more.

When he turned sharply and walked down the hall to his bedroom, she felt a sickening sensation of loss. How foolish she'd been to dream they might have a new beginning.

Sinking onto the sofa, she opened the black box and let

out a pleased cry when a necklace and earrings of rubies and diamonds exploded in fiery brilliance. He'd tucked his business card inside the box. On the back of it, scrawled in bold black ink, she read, "For my beautiful wife."

Tears filled her eyes as she hesitantly touched the necklace. She quickly brushed the dampness away. The necklace was exquisite. Nobody had ever given her anything half so lovely.

In the next breath, she told herself the gift meant nothing. He was wealthy. It was for show. He'd bought the jewels to impress Murray Oil's clients, stockholders and employees. He'd probably had someone pick them up for her. The gift wasn't personal.

"Do you like it?" Tall and dark, he stood in the doorway looking gravely handsome in his elegant black suit.

"It's too beautiful," she whispered. "You shouldn't have, but thank you."

"Then stand up, and I'll help you put it on. You have no idea how many necklaces I looked at. Nothing seemed right until I found this one."

"You shopped for it yourself?"

"Indeed. Who could I possibly trust to select the right gift for my bride? The wrong necklace could overpower you."

He let her secure the earrings to her ears before he lifted the necklace from the black velvet box and fastened it around her neck.

At the warmth of his fingertips against her nape, her skin tingled and her heart beat wildly. Was it possible to have an orgasm from sheer longing?

"With your dark hair, I thought rubies would become you, and they do," he said, staring so long at the sparkle on her slim neck his gaze made her skin burn. "I imagined you wearing them and nothing else."

In spite of herself, she giggled. *This was more like the homecoming she'd fantasized about.* In another moment, he would kiss her.

He stepped back to admire her and shot her an answering grin. Why, oh, why hadn't he kissed her?

She pursed her lips, touched her hand to her throat.

His face grew guarded again; his lips set in that firm line she'd come to dread. Instead of taking her in his arms, he backed away almost violently. "Shall we go?" he said, his tone rough and deliberately impersonal.

Cut to the quick, she didn't dare look at him as she nodded. During the short drive, he didn't speak to her again.

As soon as they arrived at the party, he put his arm around her as executives and clients rushed up and surrounded him, all clamoring to congratulate Quinn on his successes in London.

Black silk rustling, Cristina was among the first who hurried to his side. Barely managing a cool smile for Kira, she placed a bejeweled, exquisitely manicured hand on Quinn's cheek with practiced ease and kissed him lightly.

"I'm *so* proud of you," she gushed in a low, intimate tone. "I knew you'd pull it off. See—everybody loves you now. Worries over."

Clearly, he'd taken the time to inform *her* personally of his successes.

"So the deal went well?" Kira whispered into his ear when the lovely Cristina glided away.

He nodded absently as he continued shaking everybody's hand.

"Why didn't you tell me?"

"You know now, don't you?"

"But I'm your wife…"

"Unwillingly, as you keep reminding me. Which is why

I've been working hard not to burden you with too much attention."

Stung, her eyes burning and her heart heavy, she turned away. Why did it hurt that he saw no need to share the things that mattered to him when she'd known all along their marriage was for show?

She was sure he had a duty to mingle, so she was surprised when Quinn stayed by her side. When she noticed a dark-skinned man talking animatedly to her family, she asked Quinn who he was.

"Habib."

"The man you were talking to after we made love that first time?"

He nodded. "I thought you two had met…at the wedding."

"No, but we've talked on the phone this past week. Why did he think you should marry Jaycee instead of me?"

"Whatever he thought, he was wrong. What difference does it make now?"

"My mother told me today that I was adopted."

When Quinn's blue eyes darkened, she sensed that he knew more than he wanted to let on.

"Something you said that morning made me wonder if you and he somehow knew that," she persisted.

He stiffened warily.

"I thought that if you had known, maybe you assumed my family cared more about her…and maybe that was why Habib concurred with my father that she was the better choice…?"

"Habib's research did indicate a partiality on your father's part for Jacinda."

Her chest constricted. That truth was one of the reasons being loved in her own right by her husband was something that was beginning to matter to Kira more than anything.

"I preferred you from the first," he countered.

He kept saying that. Could she dare to believe him?

"Doesn't that count for something?" he asked.

"Our marriage was a business deal."

"So you keep reminding me."

"You only married me to make taking over Murray Oil go more smoothly, and now that you've made a place for yourself, your need for me is at an end."

"I'll decide when my need for you is at end. What do you say we end this depressing conversation and dance?" He took her hand. "Shall we?"

"You don't really want to dance with me— I'm just—"

"Don't put yourself down," he growled as he pulled her into his hard arms. "You're my wife."

"So, dancing with me at the company party is expected?" she said.

"I suppose." His grip strengthening, he smiled grimly down at her. "Did it ever occur to you that I might want to dance with you even if it wasn't expected?"

She was aware of people watching them and reminded herself that he was only dancing with her to make the guests believe their marriage was real.

From a corner, her laughing parents and a smiling Jaycee watched them, too. Looking at them, so happy together, Kira felt left out, as usual. Even being in Quinn's arms, knowing she was pregnant with his child, gave her no joy. How could it? Had he touched her other than for public viewing, or shown her any affection since he'd returned? Their marriage was a business deal to him, and one that wasn't nearly as important as the one he'd just concluded in London.

"Quit thinking dark, mutinous thoughts, and just dance," he whispered against her ear. "Relax. Enjoy. You're very beautiful, you know, and I'd seize any excuse to hold you in my arms."

Despite her determination to resist his appeal, his words, his nearness and his warm breath against her earlobe had her blood beating wildly.

She knew it was illogical, but being held in his arms reassured her. Soon she almost forgot dancing with him was just for show. Everyone in the gilded room blurred except her handsome husband.

They didn't speak again, but his eyes lingered on her lips as the music washed through her. Did he want to kiss her? She wanted it so much, she felt sick with longing. Surely he knew it. If so, he gave no indication, and, after a while, all the spinning about began to make her feel dizzy and much too hot.

She didn't want to be sick. Not now…not when he was finally holding her, when he seemed almost happy to be with her. Still, she couldn't take another step or she'd faint.

"I need some air," she whispered.

"All right." He led her round along the shadowy edges of the room until they came to a pair of tall French doors that opened onto a balcony overlooking the sparkling city. Gallantly, he pulled her outside. The night was mild, pleasant even. Once they were alone, his grip around her tightened in concern and he pressed her close.

"You look so strained and pale. Are you sure you're okay?"

She gulped in a breath of air. And then another. "I'm perfectly fine," she lied, believing that surely in a minute or two she would be.

"Obviously, even being in my arms is an ordeal."

"No!"

"You don't have to lie. I know well enough that I've given you ample reason to dislike me."

"I don't dislike you."

"But you don't like me. How could you? I was your father's enemy."

"Quinn—"

"No, hear me out. Since the island, I've kept my distance in order to make our marriage less onerous to you. I know I pushed you into this situation too hard and too fast, and I took advantage of you the night of the storm. I'm not proud of that. But do you have any idea how difficult it's been to stay away from you ever since?

"I wanted to give you your precious space and time to get used to our arrangement. I prayed that a week's separation would give me the strength to resist you when I returned," he muttered. "So, I didn't call you from London, and when I came home, I tried to be the cold husband you desire. But after our days apart, when you looked so ethereal and beautiful in your flashy red dress, my vow not to touch you drove me crazy. God help me, ever since the first day I saw you at your parents' ranch, you've obsessed me."

"But I don't desire a cold husband. I've wanted you, too," she whispered, wishing her feet felt a little steadier beneath her. Despite the fresh air, she was beginning to feel light-headed again.

"You have?"

Whatever encouragement he sought in her eyes, he found. Instantly, his lips were on hers, but when he crushed her closer, holding her tightly and kissing her, her dizziness returned in a sickening rush.

"I've wanted you so much," he murmured. "Missed you so much. You have no idea. Darlin', tell me you missed me, at least a little?"

Her heart beat violently even as she gulped in another breath. "Of course I did," she managed to say even as his dear face blurred and the walls of the building and the twinkling lights beneath them whirled dizzyingly like bright colors dancing in a kaleidoscope.

She willed herself to be strong, to fight the dizziness. "I did… But there's something I have to tell you, Quinn. Something…wonderful."

Little blue stars whirred. *Not good.* On the next beat the bottom dropped out of her tummy, and try as she might to save herself by gulping in mouthfuls of air, she couldn't get her breath.

"Quinn—"

Her hands, which had been pushing frantically against his hard chest, lost their strength. She was falling into a heavy darkness that was hot and swirling and all-enveloping.

The last thing she saw was Quinn's anxious face as his arms closed around her.

Fourteen

When Kira regained consciousness, Quinn was leaning over her in a small room, pressing a cool rag to her brow. To his right, a tall blond man with an air of grave authority had a finger pressed to her wrist while he studied his watch.

"Dennis is a doctor, and he wants me to ask you if...if you could possibly be pregnant," Quinn said.

"I wanted to tell...you. First thing... I really did."

"What?"

"Yes!" She blushed guiltily as Quinn stared down at her. "Yes. I'm pregnant. "I...I think that's why I got too hot while we were dancing. I've been having morning sickness while you were gone."

"That's why you were so pale. Why didn't you call me? Or tell me when I got home?" Quinn's hand tightened on her arm, and his expression grew grim. "Because you were unhappy about the baby? Were you planning to end the pregnancy without telling me?"

"No!" she exclaimed, horrified.

Quinn turned to the doctor and grilled him about her condition. The man quickly reassured him that her pulse and blood pressure were just fine. Still, he advised that she see her own doctor the next day, just to make sure.

"We're going home," Quinn said. "You're going to bed. No wonder I thought you looked thin. You should have told me."

"I was going to…"

"When?" he demanded so coldly she couldn't answer him.

That was the last word either of them said until they reached his loft. In the car, he gripped the steering wheel with clenched fists, while his profile seemed fashioned of unyielding granite. Never once did he look her way. Deliberately, he shut her out. The walls between them thickened and grew taller. Would she ever be able to reach him again?

Once inside the loft, he lingered in the crimson shower of light by the door while she fled to the master bedroom.

Alone in the vast room, she stared at the bed they'd shared. Silently, she kicked off her heels and pulled off the red dress and then slipped into a frothy white nightgown.

This wasn't the way she'd imagined telling him about the baby.

The rubies on her neck felt heavy, unbearable, but when she went to undo the clasp, her fingers shook too badly for her to manage it. The weight on her heart was even heavier. How could he have thought, even for one second, she might want to end her pregnancy? How could she go to bed when heartbreak was suffocating her?

She had to talk to him, to at least try to make things

right. Without remembering to grab a robe, she raced to the huge living room. It was empty, so she tiptoed back down the hall to his bedroom door, which he'd shut against her. She called his name, softly at first. When he didn't answer, she knocked.

His door swung open and he stood before her, his powerful, bare-chested body backlit by the lamp on his nightstand. He looked so glorious, she caught her breath. For a long moment, she could only stare at his bronzed muscles with bemused fascination. He was so fit and hard. If only she could throw herself into his arms and tell him she loved him and his baby.

But she knew he didn't want her love.

"I want this baby, and I was going to tell you," she whispered.

She watched his magnificent muscles cord as he pushed the door wider. "When?" he muttered roughly, disbelieving her.

"Just before I passed out at the party. I wanted to tell you in person, and… It was just that I was scared," she continued breathlessly. "I—I…couldn't believe you'd want my baby, too."

"Our baby," he corrected in a tight tone. "Couldn't the baby give us something more positive to build on?"

"How? If you regret marrying me. And blame our child for trapping you into a permanent involvement with a woman you don't want.

"Quinn, if you'd planned to dissolve our marriage after your takeover of Murray Oil, you don't have to stay with me because of this. I hope you know that. This doesn't have to change the businesslike nature of our arrangement."

He sucked in a breath. "Damn it. Are you ever going to quit telling me what I feel?"

"But isn't that…how you feel?"

For a long moment he was silent. "Would you listen to me for once, instead of being so sure you've got me pegged?"

"Yes. All right."

After another lengthy interval, his expression softened. "I guess I'm a little scared by your news," he said simply.

"Because you know our marriage isn't real?"

His mouth tensed. "No! Because babies are a lifetime commitment. Because they are so little…and so helpless. Because they know how to turn their parents into doting sots—and they do it with charm, in no time flat. Anything could happen to a baby." He caught her hand, and when she didn't struggle, he pulled her into his arms. "Or to you… while you're pregnant. I couldn't bear it." He kissed her brow.

It was bliss to be in his arms.

So he didn't love her, couldn't love anybody. But he cared. She was sure he cared, at least a little. He was holding her as if he did.

"But nothing will happen because we'll take good care of the baby…and me," she said reassuringly.

"My father was strong, and he died. We're all only a heartbeat away from death." There was so much grief and passion in his voice she felt hot tears sting the back of her eyelids.

"Which is why we have to live each moment to the fullest," she whispered. In a burst of tenderness, she raised her fingertips to stroke his temples in consolation. "We don't have a second to waste. We might as well be dead if we're afraid to live." To love, she wanted to add.

Quinn's arms tightened around her. He lowered his face and this time it was her mouth he sought. When he found it, he kissed her long and deeply. She opened her lips and sighed. She'd wanted him to kiss her like this for hours, days. Maybe that was why she couldn't help shivering in delight and giving him everything—all her love, even her soul—when she kissed him back.

"Oh, Kira…" For an endless time, he couldn't seem to stop kissing her. Then, suddenly, he let her go and jerked free of her embrace.

"Forgive me. I forgot—you don't want me pawing you. That's what made you sick, earlier." His dark face was flushed and his breathing ragged.

"No… I told you… I've had morning sickness. Only sometimes it's not just in the morning."

"Go to your own room. We can talk tomorrow." Even as his harsh rejection wounded, his eyes continued to hungrily devour her.

He wanted her. He was pushing her away *because* he desired her so much. And because she'd made him promise not to sleep with her.

She'd been wrong, impossible from the first. She'd missed him while he was away. She was carrying his child.

Everything had changed for them.

If she had to beg, she would.

"Don't make me sleep alone tonight," she pleaded. "Because I won't sleep. I'll just lie there…wanting you."

"I won't sleep, either. Still, in the morning you'll regret it if you don't go." His expression darkened. "Like you did before…on the island."

But she hadn't regretted it. He had.

"I don't think so," she said. "You did say we should focus on the positive…for the baby's sake. Am I right?"

His sensual mouth quirked ever so charmingly, and the heat in his gaze soon had her bones melting.

"How do you make me break every rule that allowed me to survive during my long, dark years of grief?"

"I get that you don't want to love anybody ever again.

Especially not me," she whispered. "But I'm not asking for your love tonight."

When he would have protested, she sealed his lips with a fingertip. "I'm not asking for anything you can't give. I just want to be with you."

"My father loved my mother too much, and…she destroyed him…when she left. I can't help thinking you're just waiting for the right moment to walk out."

Don't you know how much I love you? Don't you know that if only you loved me, I would never leave you?

Her knees were so weak with desire, she could barely stand. No way did she possess the courage to voice her true thoughts. She was afraid they would only drive him further away.

Her hold on him was tenuous, and only sexual. She had to accept that, use it and hope that someday she could build on that foundation.

Reaching toward him, she splayed her fingertips against his massive chest. Flesh and bone and sinew felt solid and warm beneath her open palm. When she ran her fingers over his nipples and through the dark hair that matted his torso, he groaned, which pleased her.

"Kira. Darlin'." On a shuddering sigh, he pulled her close and teased her lips and jawline with his mouth and tongue.

Lifting her, he carried her to the bed. There, he slid off his belt and slacks and pushed her nightgown down her shoulders. As it pooled onto the floor, he pulled her against him and pushed inside her slick satin warmth. Riding their mutual passion, they let it carry them like a charging black steed, faster and faster, until they soared together in torrid surrender. Afterward, as she held on to him, her sated body melted into his.

"You've ruined me," he whispered.

"Whiner," she teased.

"Seriously. I'll never be able to move again," he said.

She laughed. "Sure you will. And it better be sooner than you think. Because I'm going to be wanting more... very soon. You've neglected me...you know."

"Have I now? And whose fault was that, darlin' Kira?"

For an entire hour, he held her against his body as if she was precious to him. When she kissed his rough cheek, his throat, his nipples, he muttered huskily, "You weren't kidding, were you?"

"I've missed you."

"Slave driver."

But he smiled and ran his hands through her hair as he pulled her close.

This time his love was sweeter, and slower, and afterward, when he kissed her belly gently, he showed her that his intense passion included their precious child.

"So, you want my baby, do you?" he whispered.

"So much, too much," she admitted in a breathless whisper as she pressed his dark head against her flat stomach. "More than anything. In fact, I hope the baby's a boy and that he looks just like you."

He laughed in husky delight and nuzzled her tummy with his feverish lips. "Be careful what you wish for. He'll be a handful, I assure you."

"I can't wait."

When he held her close like this and was so teasingly affectionate, she could almost forget he didn't love her, that he never could. She could almost forget how inadequate and uncertain she'd always felt.

Almost...

He was a handsome billionaire, who could have any woman he wanted. What could she do to hold him?

Nestled in his arms, she fell into a restless sleep and

dreamed. She was a child again, standing beside her parents as they cheered Jaycee and her basketball team to victory. Then she was sitting in her room alone. The house was empty because her mother and father had driven Jaycee to a slumber party.

Older now, Kira was walking across the stage at Princeton where she'd graduated with honors. As she posed for photographs, she smiled brightly through her disappointment. None of her family was in the audience because Jaycee had a conflicting high school event. The picture was all they'd have to remember this huge milestone in Kira's life.

"Remember to smile," her mother had commanded over the phone. "You never smile." A pause. "Oh, how I wish I could be there to see you graduate!"

"Couldn't Daddy stay with Jaycee?"

"You know your father. He's no good at those high school functions without me."

The dream darkened into a nightmare. Quinn was standing in a shower of crimson light, holding Cristina against his long, lean body. "I have to marry *her,* don't you understand? I don't want to. You're the one who's special to me. Don't ever forget that my marriage to her is strictly business. You're the woman who really matters. Who will always matter. Nothing will change between us. You'll see."

Then he kissed Cristina as those awful words repeated themselves in her mind. "Strictly business..."

Kira woke up crying that phrase even as Quinn wrapped his arms around her and held her close.

"Hush. It's okay, baby. You were only dreaming."

Was she? Or were her dreams where she faced the harsh truths she denied when awake?

"I'm fine," she murmured, pushing him away. "You

don't have to comfort me. I can take care of myself—just like I always have. I didn't ask you to love me—did I?"

"No, you damn sure didn't."

Strictly business.

God, if only Quinn could feel that way, too, maybe then he'd survive this nightmare.

As soon as Kira's breathing had become regular again and Quinn was sure she was asleep, he'd tossed his own covers aside and shot out of bed.

Groping clumsily for his slacks on the dark floor, he yanked them on and stalked out of the bedroom in bare feet. When he got to the bar, he splashed a shot of vodka into a glass.

Strictly business.

Damn her! Not that he didn't feel sorry for her, because he did. Even now, her stricken cries echoed in his mind. She was no happier than he was.

He'd been right to think she'd regret the sex. So, why the hell had she slept with him when he'd given her an out?

He'd never figure her out. She might regret what had happened, but he couldn't. She'd been too sweet, and he'd craved her too desperately. Hell, it embarrassed him to think of how needy he'd felt all week without her in London.

Frowning as he stared into his glass, he remembered how he'd grabbed his cell phone at least a dozen times in his eagerness to call her, only to shove it back in his pocket. All he'd wanted was to hear her soft voice. Without her, he'd felt cut off, alone, alienated in a city he usually enjoyed.

Once in San Antonio, he'd rushed home. And when he'd seen her, he'd wanted nothing except to sweep her into his arms and kiss her endlessly. But she'd been pale and withdrawn.

Every day his obsession for her increased. If she could not reciprocate, they were shackled together on the same fatal course his own parents had traveled. He would not endure that kind of marriage.

His father had given his mother everything, and it hadn't been enough.

He would not make the same mistake.

Fifteen

Quinn's side of the bed was ice-cold.

Nothing had changed.

He was gone.

It wasn't the first time Kira had woken up alone in Quinn's bed, but this morning, she felt needier than usual. Maybe because of what they'd shared the night before, or maybe because of her bad dreams, she wanted a good-morning kiss. And maybe breakfast together punctuated with a lot more kisses.

But he'd left her for work, which was all-important to him. Hadn't business been the sole reason he'd married her?

To him, last night must have been about sex and nothing more. She'd known that, hadn't she? Still, as she lay in bed, her body sore from making love, she felt lonely. Would it always be like this?

Stretching, she rolled onto his side of the bed where his

scent lingered and hugged his pillow. Then, realizing what an idiot she was, she hurled his pillow at the wall. It struck an etching, which crashed to the floor.

Footsteps in the corridor brought a quick blush to her face.

"Mrs. Sullivan? Is that you? Do you need my assistance?" Jason sounded so stiff and formal, she cringed. She wanted her husband, not some uptight houseman with high-class British airs.

"I'm fine," she cried.

How was she going to get from Quinn's room to hers in her sheer nightie without Jason seeing her wrapped in a blanket? Such an encounter would be embarrassing for both of them.

When five minutes passed without another sound, she cracked the door. There was no sign of him, so she ripped a blanket off the bed, covered herself and shot down the hall on flying tiptoes. Once inside her bedroom, she bolted the door.

As she dressed, taking her time because it was hours before she needed to be at Betty's, she turned on the television. Murray Oil and the EU deal were all over the news.

Both the local news channels and the national ones were full of stories about Quinn's heady successes. In too many shots, a beaming Cristina stood so close to Quinn the pair seemed joined at the hip. Why hadn't Quinn told her that Cristina had gone to London with him?

Cristina worked for him. Surely he'd taken other executives. It was no big deal.

But in her fragile mood, and after her dream last night, it felt like a big deal to her.

You can't blame a man for something you dreamed!

Maybe not, but she still had to ask him about Cristina and his reasons for taking the woman to London. So, when

he phone rang, she rushed to pick it up, hoping it was
Quinn.

"Hello!" she said a little too brightly.

"Kira? You don't sound like yourself."

The critical male tone was very familiar. Still, because
he was focused on Quinn, it took her a second to place
he voice. Then it came to her: Gary Whitehall, her former
oss.

"Hi, Gary."

"Are you still looking for a job?"

"I am," she said.

"Even though you're Quinn Sullivan's wife?"

"Yes, even though. He's a very busy man, and I love
oing what I'm trained to do."

"Well, Maria is retiring because she needs more time to
elp her daughter. The minute she told me she wanted to
lay grandmother, well, naturally, we all thought of you."

She lifted a brow. *And Quinn.*

"You could have your old job back… Although, like I
aid, I wasn't at all sure you'd be interested now that you're
he Mrs. Sullivan."

"Well, I am, so…this is wonderful news."

"Then you'll make yourself available for a meeting? No
urry, though. Don't want to pressure you."

"I'm available. In fact, I'm free for an hour or two this
fternoon."

They agreed upon a time and hung up.

The call boosted her mood until she remembered how
Quinn had rushed off to work this morning without even
goodbye. Until she remembered what a gorgeous couple
e and Cristina had made on television. They were both
o stylish and good-looking. They had business concerns
n common, too.

With an effort, she quit thinking about Cristina and refocused on Gary's offer. She was glad Gary had called, even if it was her marriage to Quinn that had made her more attractive as a job applicant.

On a whim, she decided to call Quinn and run the job idea by him just to see what he'd say.

Oh, be honest, Kira, you just want to hear his sexy voice and distract him from Cristina.

Kira made the call, only to be deflated when his secretary told her, "I'll have him return your call. He's in a meeting."

"With whom?"

"Cristina Gold. They're taking a last look at the contracts for the EU deal before everything is finalized."

Don't ask a question if you don't want the answer.

"Would you please tell him…that I'll be on my cell."

"Are you all right, Mrs. Sullivan?"

"I'm fine," she whispered as she hung up.

Perfectly fine.

Clutching the phone to her breast, she sank onto her bed. She didn't feel fine. She felt more uncertain than ever.

Leave it alone. Cristina works for him. That's all there is to it. Go to Betty's. Do the interview with Gary. Forget your stupid nightmare.

But being pregnant had her feeling highly emotional. She couldn't leave it alone. She had to see him. After last night, she had to know how he felt.

Dressing hurriedly, she was in his office in less than an hour. The same beautiful blonde secretary who'd greeted her on her first visit greeted her again, more warmly this time.

"Mr. Sullivan told me you two are expecting a baby. He sounded so happy about it. Congratulations."

"Thank you."

"Would you like coffee? Or a soda?"

"I just want to talk to my husband. He didn't call me back, and since I was in the neighborhood…"

"I'm afraid he's still going over those contracts."

"With Miss Gold?"

The young woman nodded. "I'm afraid the documents are long and very complicated. A mistake could cost millions. Miss Gold is one of our attorneys, you see. She had several concerns."

"Please tell him I'm here."

After the young woman buzzed him, she looked up almost immediately. "He says he'll see you. Now."

Intending to lead her down the hall, she arose, but Kira held up a hand. "I remember the way."

When Kira reached his office, Cristina was just exiting with a thick sheaf of documents. She tossed Kira a tight smile. Behind Cristina, Quinn leaned negligently against the doorjamb.

When he opened the door, Kira said, "I hope I'm not interrupting."

"Glad that meeting's over. And doubly glad to see you." He shut the door. "I needed a break."

Despite the welcoming words, when their eyes met, she felt a sudden unbearable tension coming from him.

"Sorry I left so early this morning, but I had a couple of urgent texts."

"From Cristina?"

"One was. Unfortunately, I still have a lot of balls in the air related to the EU deal," he said.

"No problem."

"You look upset." His voice was flat.

"I didn't realize Cristina went to London with you… until I saw some of the news coverage on television."

A cynical black brow lifted. "I took a team of ten. She

was part of the team. She's very talented at what she does or I never would have hired her."

"Not only is she talented, but she's beautiful, too."

He stood very still. "I imagine her looks are part of why she made it into so many of the TV shots. Look, there's no need for you to be jealous of her...if that's what this is."

"I'm not."

"I'm married to you, and whether you believe it or not that means something to me."

What did it really mean if he could never love her?

"Since you obviously want to know more about Cristina and me," he began in the maddening, matter-of-fact tone of a lawyer presenting his case, "I'll clarify our relationship. We dated briefly. The press gave our romance more attention than it deserved.

"Then she broke up with me—for another man with whom she's still seriously involved. At the time, she complained I never had time for her. He did. Naturally, I was angry, but since then I've realized she was right."

"A vengeful man might have held what she did against her," she said coolly. "Why did you hire her?"

"We worked together on several projects before we dated. She will do a lot for Murray Oil."

"So, as always, business is all-important to you? Does nothing else ever matter? Not even your own injured feelings?"

He shrugged. "They weren't that injured. I got over her pretty quickly."

Would he get over Kira and be this matter-of-fact about it? At the thought, Kira cringed.

"Business will always be an important part of my life. I don't deny that. It's part of who I am. I hired her...before I met you." He paused. "What is it you want from me this morning, Kira?"

"Right. I'm interrupting you. You're a busy man. You probably have many more important meetings to get through today. All those balls in the air. And here I am, your pregnant, overly emotional wife needing reassurance."

He studied her warily. "What do you want, Kira?"

Why couldn't she be as cool and logical as he was? Because everything in her life was out of balance. She was pregnant and feeling needy. There were too many unanswered questions in their relationship, and she was still reeling from the discovery that she'd been adopted.

She wanted to belong somewhere, to someone. She wanted to matter to *Quinn*. If she'd been more important to him, wouldn't he have kept her in the loop while he was gone? Wouldn't he have shared more details concerning his oil deal?

"I guess I want the impossible," she blurted out. "I want a real marriage."

"Now you want a real marriage, when all along you've said that's the last thing you want? Last night you woke up crying from some dream, apparently about me, demanding 'strictly business.' You pushed me away as if you wanted nothing to do with me. If I give you space it's wrong. If I push myself on you it's wrong."

"I know I'm not making sense," she said. "Our marriage was never based on love, mutual understanding or anything that makes up a true partnership. I guess I'm upset because…because I don't know… I just know I can't go on like this!"

"As soon as I complete this deal, I'll have more time…"

"How will that matter if you don't want the same kind of marriage I do? Now, maybe because of the baby and finding out I was adopted, I have this huge need for things to be right between us. I want more. I've wanted more my whole life. I don't want to feel left out anymore. Most of all, I want to count to my husband."

"If you wanted to belong in this marriage, then why did you tell me from the first that you didn't want to sleep with me?"

"I guess to protect myself...from ever feeling like I feel now—needy...confused. I knew this marriage was only a business deal for you. I didn't want to get my heart broken," she whispered.

"What are you saying?"

"What we have isn't enough. Not for me...or for you."

"You're pregnant. We can't just walk away from each other. It's not about you and me anymore, or even Murray Oil. We have a child to think about now."

"That's all the more reason I don't want us trapped in a loveless marriage. I want a husband who can love me. I want my child to grow up in a loving home. After the deal you just made, the executives at Murray Oil trust you. You don't need to be married to me anymore. You can divorce me and date somebody who understands you, someone who can make you happy...someone like Cristina."

"Damn it. I don't want a divorce. Or Cristina. Like I said—if you'd ever once listen to me—she's practically engaged."

"But you don't love me..."

"Well, I damn sure don't love anyone else. And I'm not lusting after anybody else. I'm focused solely on you! You're very important to me, Kira. Vital. Still, it's true that I'm not sure I'll ever be capable of loving anyone—even you. Maybe I've been hard and dark and driven for too long."

"Well, I want a man who will commit his heart to me, or I want out."

"Okay," he said in a tone that was cold, infuriatingly

logical and final. "Now that our marriage has served its purpose, you want out. Well, I don't want out, and I'm not ready to let you go. But if that's what you want, I won't hold you against your will any longer."

"What?"

"I'll give you what you say you want. You're free to leave. But understand this—I intend to take an active role in raising our child."

"Of course," she whispered, feeling shattered.

"Then so be it," he said.

He stared at her, waiting for her to walk out the door, and, for a brief moment, his guard fell. She saw longing and pain flash in his eyes.

Suddenly, she realized just how much she'd wanted him to fight for her, for them.

After stumbling blindly out of his office, she sat behind the wheel of her car, clenching her keys in her hand. All her life she'd wanted someone to fight for her, someone to put her first. She'd had a right to push for more from her marriage.

He wasn't willing to fight for her as he'd fought for his oil deal in London, so she would do the fighting.

She would fight for her self-respect, and she would teach their child to fight for his, too.

Kira had been in no condition to be interviewed by Gary the afternoon she'd parted from Quinn, so she'd rescheduled.

Two miserable days later, she still didn't feel strong enough, but here she sat, facing Gary across his wide, cluttered desk in his flashy corner office that overlooked the museum grounds and the busy street that fronted the modern building.

If only she could stop thinking about Quinn and how

bereft she'd felt ever since he'd agreed to end their marriage.

Concentrating on Gary, who wasn't the most fascinating man, was difficult. Lately, everything had been difficult. Returning to Quinn's gorgeous loft, packing the beautiful clothes that she would no longer need and then moving back into her cramped apartment with her dead plants and resentful cat had been full of emotional hurdles.

Rudy wouldn't sit on her lap or use his scratching post. Only this morning he'd peed on her pillow just to show her how much he resented being abandoned.

"Quit feeling sorry for yourself! I'm the one who got married and pregnant...and separated," she'd yelled at him.

Swishing his tail, he'd flattened his ears and stalked indifferently to his bowl where he'd howled for more tuna.

She tried to pay attention to Gary, she really did, but her mind constantly wandered to her miserable new separated state and to Quinn and how cold he'd been right before he'd watched her walk away.

Suddenly, she found Gary's droning insufferable and longed to be anywhere else, even home alone with her sullen cat. If she didn't interrupt Gary, he might easily rant on for another half an hour.

"Gary, this is all very fascinating, but I need to ask a question."

He frowned.

"Is this job offer contingent on me remaining married to Quinn?"

"What?"

"Let me be blunt."

His mouth tightened. "You do that so well."

"Quinn and I have separated. Do you still want me for this job? "

His face fell. "Separated?" Flushing, he pushed himself

back from his desk. "Well, that does change things." Recovering quickly, he ran a nervous hand through his hair. "Still, I want you to work here, of course."

Her voice was equally silky as she leaned toward him. "*Of course.* I'm so glad we understand each other."

A few minutes later he hastily concluded the interview. "I'll call you," he said.

She left, wondering if he would.

As she stood on the curb outside the museum, about to cross the street, Jaycee called her on her cell.

"How are things going?"

"I've been better," Kira replied. "The interview with Gary went okay, I guess."

"And Rudy?"

"He peed on my pillow this morning."

"Well, you abandoned him. He's still mad at you."

"I guess. Hold on—"

Pressing the phone against her ear, she looked both ways to cross the street. But just as she jumped into the crosswalk a motorcycle made a left turn, going too fast.

She felt a surge of panic, but it was too late. In the next moment, she was hurled into the air.

It was true what they said about your life flashing before your eyes.

She saw Quinn's darkly handsome face and knew suddenly, without a doubt, that she loved him.

It didn't matter that he could never love her. Or maybe she knew, on some deep level, that he must love her, too—at least a little.

She remembered all the times he'd looked at her and she'd felt her soul join to his.

She'd been an idiot to walk out on the man she loved, to

abandon a man so afraid of love that he denied what was in his own heart. He needed her.

She wanted to get up and run back to his office. She wanted to beg him for another chance. But when she tried to sit up, her body felt as if it were made of concrete.

Someone knelt over her, but she couldn't see his face.

"Quinn," she cried. "I want Quinn."

The man spoke, but she couldn't hear what he said.

Then everything went black.

"A Jerry Sullivan is here to see you," Quinn's secretary informed him crisply. "Says he's family."

"Show him in," Quinn ordered in a dull voice as he set the lightning whelk Kira had given him back on the shelf. "He's my uncle. He'll want coffee with cream and sugar."

Uncle Jerry didn't wait for Quinn's secretary to return with his coffee before he pounced.

"Sorry to interrupt you, but I just heard you separated from your beautiful wife. I'd ask you to tell me it isn't true, but since you look like something my dog dragged in from the gutter, I won't bother."

"Good to see you, too, Uncle J."

"What the hell did you do to drive her away?"

"I never should have married her in the first place."

"If you let her go, you'll be making the biggest mistake of your life. You've already wasted too many years of your life alone."

"Let me be, why don't you?"

"You're still in love with her. I can see it!"

"The hell I am. Did anybody ever tell you to mind your own business?"

"Sure. You. Plenty of times. Good thing I've got better sense than to listen to the likes of an upstart nephew who doesn't have a clue about what's good for him."

"I think some men are better off single. And I'm probably one of them."

"Bull. I saw the way you were with her. You're like your father. He was the most loving man I ever knew."

"And what did it get him—other than a broken heart and an early grave?"

"You're not your father. Kira's not Esther. Kira's the real thing. Esther was a beautiful woman who knew how to play your dad. And, yes, your dad foolishly loved her with all his heart—just like he loved you. But when you get down to it, even when you're wrong about the people you love, loving is still the best way to live. That's why we still miss Kade. He loved us all so much!"

"My father killed himself because my mother left him."

"You'll never make me believe that! Kade wouldn't ever deliberately walk out on you. You were everything to him. His death was an accident."

"Uncle Jerry, thanks for coming by."

"Great. Now you're giving me the brush-off."

"I know you mean well...but I'm a grown man—"

"Who has the right to screw up his life royally and who's doing a damn good job of it."

"If you've said your piece, I've got work to do."

"You've always got work to do! Maybe it's time you got a life." Uncle Jerry smiled grimly. "Okay, I'll leave you to it, not that it's any fun watching my favorite nephew walk out on the best thing that ever happened to him."

"I didn't walk out on her! Damn it! She left me!"

"So, quit sulking, and go after her!"

"If only it were that easy!"

"Trust me—it is. The only thing stopping you is your damn arrogance."

"Get the hell out of here!"

Holding a silver tray with a coffee cup, Quinn's secretary pushed the door open and would have entered except Quinn held up a hand. "Uncle Jerry won't be having coffee after all. He's leaving."

For some time after his uncle had gone, Quinn sat in his office and seethed. Slowly, as he cooled down, everything the older man had said began replaying in his mind. Since his father's death, Uncle Jerry was the one person Quinn had been able to count on.

Quinn walked over to the shelf where he'd placed the lightning whelk. How full of hope he'd felt when she'd given it to him. He remembered her shining eyes, her glowing beauty.

Turning away, he grabbed his cell phone. For a long moment he just held it.

Quinn didn't just want to call Kira for his own selfish reasons. He was genuinely worried about her and the baby. The longer he went without talking to her, the more worried he grew. Would it be so wrong to call just to make sure she and the baby were all right? Would it? Even if they never got back together, she was the mother of his future child.

Swallowing his pride, he lifted his phone and punched in her number. As he waited for her to answer, his gut clenched.

Then, on the third ring, a man answered.

"I want Kira," Quinn thundered. "I need to speak to my wife."

"Sir, I'm so sorry. I'm terribly afraid there's been an accident..."

The man introduced himself as someone working at the local hospital. He said something about a motorcycle hitting Kira and that Kira had been taken to his emergency room by ambulance. After getting the specifics, Quinn hung up and was grabbing his jacket and on his way to the door, when Earl Murray rang his cell phone.

Quinn picked up on the first ring. "I just heard Kira's been hurt."

"Apparently, Jaycee was talking to her when the motorcycle hit her... I don't know anything else."

"Then I'll meet you at the hospital," Quinn said. His heart was in his throat as he bolted out of his office in a dead run, praying he wouldn't be too late.

Sixteen

Quinn had never been as scared in his life as he was when he stood over Kira watching the IV drip clear liquid into her veins. Her narrow face had the awful grayish tint Quinn had seen only one time before—on his father's face as he'd lain in a pool of his own blood.

"Tell me she's going to be all right. Tell me the baby's all right."

"I've told you," the doctor repeated patiently. "Apparently, she was thrown onto the pavement, but seems to have suffered only a concussion and a few bruises. After a night or two of rest, she and the baby will be fine. She's one lucky young lady."

"You're sure?" For some reason, the facts weren't sticking in Quinn's head as they usually did.

"As sure as I can be under the circumstances."

"When will she wake up?"

"Like I told you before—soon. You just have to be patient."

An hour later, the longest hour of Quinn's life, her long lashes fluttered. Sensing that she was struggling to focus on him, Quinn gripped her hand and leaned forward.

"Kira… Darlin'…"

"Quinn… I wanted you to come. I wanted it so much."

"Kira, you're in a hospital. You're going to be okay. The baby, too."

"I love you," she said softly. "I was such a fool."

Rather than terrifying him, those three words brought a rush of joy.

"I love you, too. More than anything." He squeezed her hand tightly. "So much it scares the hell out of me."

It had only taken her admission to make him brave enough to admit his own feelings for her.

With glistening eyes, she laughed softly. "You really love me?"

"Yes. Maybe even from the first moment I saw you. I just didn't know what had hit me." He paused. "Jaycee's here, along with your parents. We've all been so scared for you and the baby. Half out of our minds."

"They're all here, too?"

"Of course we're here," her father roared.

Kira smiled radiantly up at them. "It's almost worth getting hit by a motorcycle to have all of you all here… together, knowing…knowing that you love me."

They moved closer, circling her bed. Holding hands, they smiled down at her. "Of course we love you," her father said. "You're our girl."

"You gave us a terrible scare," her mother said. "You're very important to all of us."

"I'm so happy," Kira whispered. "I've never been happier."

"By the way," her father said, "your old boss called and said you'd better get well soon because you've got a big job at the museum waiting for you. So, no more waitressing…"

Kira smiled weakly. "I guess that's good news…but not nearly as good as all of you being here." Her grip on Quinn's hand tightened as she looked up at him. "I never, ever want to let go of you again."

"You won't have to."

Quinn needed no further encouragement to lean forward and kiss her. Very carefully, so as not to hurt her, he pressed his mouth to her lips.

As always, she gave her entire being to him, causing warmth and happiness to flow from her soul into his.

She was everything to him. He would love her and cherish her always, or at least until the last breath left his body.

"Darlin'," he whispered. "Promise me you'll never leave me again."

She nodded. "Never. I swear it. Like I said, I was a fool."

Circling his neck with her hands, she brought his face down to hers and kissed him again.

Epilogue

Kira looked across the green lawns that sloped down to cypress trees shading the sparkling river. The air stirring through the leaves was warm, while the water was clear and icy.

Kira couldn't believe her happiness. Ever since that afternoon in the hospital, when she'd awakened to Quinn and her family gathered around her bed, her happiness had grown a little every day.

Despite the pain in her shoulder and back, she'd seen the love shining in all their eyes.

Love for her.

Had it always been there? Whether it had or not, all her doubts about herself, about Quinn, about her adoption, had vanished. She'd simply known that she mattered—to all of them.

She belonged.

Knowing she was truly loved, her confidence had grown in every aspect of her life, including in her career as a curator. Naturally, Gary had been thrilled that she was to remain Mrs. Sullivan. Quinn had thrilled him even more by being most generous to the museum, stipulating with every donation that his wife be in charge of the funds.

This lazy summer afternoon on the grounds of the Sullivans' new weekend home on the Blanco was perfect for a July Fourth celebration that included friends, family and business associates. The star of the show was only a few months old.

Thomas Kade Sullivan fulfilled his mother's most fervent hopes as he sat on his red-and-blue quilt by the water, holding court. He shook his rattle while Aunt Jaycee laughed and held up a stuffed bunny rabbit. With his brilliant blue eyes, Tommy Kade was every bit as handsome as his father.

Off to one side, a band played as their guests took turns swimming in the cool waters or serving themselves barbecue.

Quinn left the men he'd been talking to and walked up to her. Grinning down at her, he circled her with his arms. Contentment made her feel soft and warm as he held her close. Never had she dreamed she'd feel this complete with anyone.

She smiled at the sight of her mother ordering the caterers about. With her illness in remission, her mother was her old formidable self. When Vera had been well enough for Kira's dad to leave her at home, Quinn had made a place for him at Murray Oil.

"Murray Oil's too big for one man to run," Quinn had said when Kira had tried to thank him.

Life was good, she thought as her husband brushed his lips against her cheek. Very good.

"Happy July Fourth," Quinn said.

"The happiest ever."

"For me, too. Because you're in my life," he murmured huskily. "You're the best thing that ever happened to me... besides Tommy Kade. And you're responsible for him, too."

"Stop. We're at a party. We have to behave."

"Maybe I don't want to behave."

He drew her away from the crowd into the shade of the towering cypress trees. Once they were hidden from their guests, he wrapped her in his arms and kissed her long and deeply.

"I love you," he whispered. "I love you, and I always will. We have a real marriage, now—wouldn't you agree?"

The most wonderful thing of all was that she knew it and accepted it—down to her bones—because she felt exactly the same way. "I would! And I love you, too," she murmured. "Oh, how I love you."

* * * * *

PASSION

For a spicier, decidedly hotter read—
this is your destination for romance!

COMING NEXT MONTH
AVAILABLE FEBRUARY 14, 2012

#2137 TO KISS A KING
Kings of California
Maureen Child

#2138 WHAT HAPPENS IN CHARLESTON...
Dynasties: The Kincaids
Rachel Bailey

#2139 MORE THAN PERFECT
Billionaires and Babies
Day Leclaire

#2140 A COWBOY IN MANHATTAN
Colorado Cattle Barons
Barbara Dunlop

#2141 THE WAYWARD SON
The Master Vintners
Yvonne Lindsay

#2142 BED OF LIES
Paula Roe

HDCNM0112

REQUEST YOUR FREE BOOKS!
2 FREE NOVELS PLUS 2 FREE GIFTS!

Harlequin

Desire

ALWAYS POWERFUL, PASSIONATE AND PROVOCATIVE

YES! Please send me 2 FREE Harlequin Desire® novels and my 2 FREE gifts (gifts are worth about $10). After receiving them, if I don't wish to receive any more books, I can return the shipping statement marked "cancel." If I don't cancel, I will receive 6 brand-new novels every month and be billed just $4.30 per book in the U.S. or $4.99 per book in Canada. That's a saving of at least 14% off the cover price! It's quite a bargain! Shipping and handling is just 50¢ per book in the U.S. and 75¢ per book in Canada.* I understand that accepting the 2 free books and gifts places me under no obligation to buy anything. I can always return a shipment and cancel at any time. Even if I never buy another book, the two free books and gifts are mine to keep forever.

225/326 HDN FEF3

Name	(PLEASE PRINT)	

Address		Apt. #

City	State/Prov.	Zip/Postal Code

Signature (if under 18, a parent or guardian must sign)

Mail to the **Reader Service:**
IN U.S.A.: P.O. Box 1867, Buffalo, NY 14240-1867
IN CANADA: P.O. Box 609, Fort Erie, Ontario L2A 5X3

Not valid for current subscribers to Harlequin Desire books.

Want to try two free books from another line?
Call 1-800-873-8635 or visit www.ReaderService.com.

* Terms and prices subject to change without notice. Prices do not include applicable taxes. Sales tax applicable in N.Y. Canadian residents will be charged applicable taxes. Offer not valid in Quebec. This offer is limited to one order per household. All orders subject to credit approval. Credit or debit balances in a customer's account(s) may be offset by any other outstanding balance owed by or to the customer. Please allow 4 to 6 weeks for delivery. Offer available while quantities last.

Your Privacy—The Reader Service is committed to protecting your privacy. Our Privacy Policy is available online at www.ReaderService.com or upon request from the Reader Service.

We make a portion of our mailing list available to reputable third parties that offer products we believe may interest you. If you prefer that we not exchange your name with third parties, or if you wish to clarify or modify your communication preferences, please visit us at www.ReaderService.com/consumerchoice or write to us at Reader Service Preference Service, P.O. Box 9062, Buffalo, NY 14269. Include your complete name and address.

HDES11B

Rhonda Nelson

SIZZLES WITH ANOTHER INSTALLMENT OF

When former ranger Jack Martin is assigned to provide security to Mariette Levine, a local pastry chef, he believes this will be an open-and-shut case. Yet the danger becomes all too real when Mariette is attacked. But things aren't always what they seem, and soon Jack's protective instincts demand he save the woman he is quickly falling for.

THE KEEPER

Available February 2012
wherever books are sold.

*Louisa Morgan loves being around children.
So when she has the opportunity to tutor bedridden Ellie,
she's determined to bring joy back into the motherless
girl's world. Can she also help Ellie's father open his
heart again? Read on for a sneak peek of*

THE COWBOY FATHER

*by Linda Ford,
available February 2012 from Love Inspired Historical.*

Why had Louisa thought she could do this job? A bubble of self-pity whispered she was totally useless, but Louisa ignored it. She wasn't useless. She could help Ellie if the child allowed it.

Emmet walked her out, waiting until they were out of earshot to speak. "I sense you and Ellie are not getting along."

"Ellie has lost her freedom. On top of that, everything is new. Familiar things are gone. Her only defense is to exert what little independence she has left. I believe she will soon tire of it and find there are more enjoyable ways to pass the time."

He looked doubtful. Louisa feared he would tell her not to return. But after several seconds' consideration, he sighed heavily. "You're right about one thing. She's lost everything. She can hardly be blamed for feeling out of sorts."

"She hasn't lost everything, though." Her words were quiet, coming from a place full of certainty that Emmet was more than enough for this child. "She has you."

"She'll always have me. As long as I live." He clenched his fists. "And I fully intend to raise her in such a way that even if something happened to me, she would never feel like I was gone. I'd be in her thoughts and in her actions every day."

Peace filled Louisa. "Exactly what my father did."

Their gazes connected, forged a single thought about fathers and daughters…how each needed the other. How sweet the relationship was.

Louisa tipped her head away first. "I'll see you tomorrow."

Emmet nodded. "Until tomorrow then."

She climbed behind the wheel of their automobile and turned toward home. She admired Emmet's devotion to his child. It reminded her of the love her own father had lavished on Louisa and her sisters. Louisa smiled as fond memories of her father filled her thoughts. Ellie was a fortunate child to know such love.

Louisa understands what both father and daughter are going through. Will her compassion help them heal—and form a new family? Find out in
THE COWBOY FATHER
by Linda Ford, available February 14, 2012.

Love Inspired Books celebrates 15 years of inspirational romance in 2012! February puts the spotlight on Love Inspired Historical, with each book celebrating family and the special place it has in our hearts. Be sure to pick up all four Love Inspired Historical stories, available February 14, wherever books are sold.

SHLIHEXP0212